P9-BJV-366

Side Out

Barbara L. Clanton

A Dragonfeather Book

Bedazzled Ink Publishing Company * Fairfield, California

© 2011 Barbara L. Clanton

All rights reserved. No part of this publication may be
reproduced or transmitted in any means, electronic or mechanical,
without permission in writing
from the publisher.

978-1-934452-65-3 paperback
978-1-934452-66-0 ebook

Library of Congress Control Number: 2011935873

A Title IX Book

Cover art
by
Tree House Studio

Dragonfeather Books
a division of
Bedazzled Ink Publishing Company
Fairfield, California
http://www.dragonfeatherbooks.com

Dedication

This work is dedicated to the Hadassah-Brandeis Institute in Waltham, Massachusetts whose important efforts illuminate the relationship between Jews and gender worldwide.

The text follows the Jewish tradition of not writing out the Lord's Name to prevent it from being defaced or erased.

Acknowledgments

It is a real privilege to be able to write stories about sports—a topic I'm passionate about, so I have to thank the gang from Dragonfeather Books at Bedazzled Ink Publishing Company for giving me the opportunity. I also want to thank Diane Rosenbaum for tweaking my understanding of Jewish culture and traditions; Ralph Mazza, Dee Starling, and Georgia Parker for letting me pick their brains about youth volleyball; and Sheri Milburn for being a faithful beta reader and friend. Thanks also go out to my family (you know who you are) for always being supportive. And lastly, but not leastly, I need to thank Jackie Weathers, my partner in life, who continually supports my efforts and who has become (almost) as big a sports' fan as I am.

Chapter 1
Corn Country

Dina Jacobs sat on the hard bleachers in the Amelia Earhart Middle School gymnasium, wishing the athletic director would wrap up her welcome speech. The volleyball tryouts should have started already. She sighed and looked around her. The gym at her old school in Hawkinsville, Long Island, New York only had one volleyball court, not three like this one. Her parents told her that everything would seem bigger in Indiana. They weren't lying. Indiana seemed to go on and on and on, and all it seemed to have was corn, corn, and more corn. Oh, and soybeans. Whatever those were.

Her mother nudged her in the side. "Are you nervous, honey?"

"A little." Dina readjusted her knee pads and pulled her jet black hair into a pony tail. She liked to keep the hair off her neck when she played, so she tacked the end of the ponytail to the back of her head with a barrette.

Dina leaned close to her mother and whispered, "All these girls in cawn country probably have nuttin' bettuh to do than play volleyball twenty-four sev."

"Cawn country?" Her mother laughed. "Honey, you've got to work on that Long Island accent of yours." She patted Dina on the knee. "You'll be fine. I'll be right here on the bleachers if you get nervous, okay? Just look back, and I'll give you a thumbs up."

"Okay."

Dr. Lewiski, the athletic director, finally stopped talking and directed the sixth graders to the court at the far end of the gym. She then called for the seventh graders to go to the middle court.

"Oh, there you go," her mother said.

Dina stood up. "Wish me luck." With her mom's well wishes, she bounded down the bleachers.

Adina Jacobs and her parents had moved to West Lafayette, Indiana in June after Dina's mother had been hired as an assistant professor of Environmental Science at Purdue University. Dina wasn't happy getting ripped away from her friends in New York, but her mother promised they'd go back to visit as often as they could. So far that hadn't happened, but then again it had only been about a month and a half since they left. School in Indiana was set to start in a week, and with volleyball tryouts for the next three days, they wouldn't get back to Long Island for a while. Maybe not even until next summer.

Dina hustled to the seventh grade court, not wanting to be the last one, and stood with the other girls. A quick count revealed about twenty-five seventh graders. There would definitely be cuts. She hoped she wasn't one of them.

"All right, girls," the seventh grade coach said, "because we have three full teams in here tonight, it's important that everyone remain focused and listen. Is that understood?"

Dina nodded along with the other girls and took a deep breath to shake out her nerves. The seventh grade coach looked more like an army sergeant than a volleyball coach with her short brown hair, dark eyes, and lack of smile. Dina exchanged a worried glance with the short girl standing next to her.

"My name is Coach Matthews, but you can call me Coach." She glanced at the clipboard in her hand. "Right now, I need you to form three straight lines for stretching." The girls looked around at each other. "Move it."

Twenty-five seventh graders burst into activity. In what seemed like forever, they finally formed three straight lines of roughly the same size. Dina, luckily, found a place to hide in the back row, although at five-foot-nine she kind of stuck out like the Empire State Building. She smiled at the short girl who had found a spot next to her.

"Let's stretch," Coach Matthews snapped.

While the coach led them through their stretching

routine, Dina snuck a peek at the girls around her. She didn't know a single one of them. The only new girls she'd met so far in Indiana were at Temple Beth Israel, and none of them went to Earhart Middle. She was all alone.

"Okay. Break into pairs," Coach Matthews said, once they were done stretching. "One ball between you."

"Wanna be my partner?" the short girl asked.

"Sure." Dina was relieved she didn't have to find a partner on her own.

The short girl grabbed a ball from the bin.

"I'm Christine Hannigan," she said when she came back.

"Nice tuh meet cha. I'm Dina. Dina Jacobs." She stuck out her hand.

Christine looked perplexed for a second at Dina's outstretched hand, but then finally shook it. "Nice to meet you, Dina. Are you new here?"

"Yeah, I just moved he-uh." They passed the ball back and forth, following the coach's instructions.

"He-uh? Where's he-uh?" Christine sounded confused.

"Heeeeere, I mean. I just moved here." She over exaggerated the proper pronunciation.

"Yeah, I can tell. Your accent is way weird." Christine smiled, and Dina knew she was teasing.

"*My* accent? No, seriously, youse guys are da ones wit duh accents." She laid it on thick.

Christine laughed again. "Where are you from anyway?"

"Whatsa matta wit you?" Dina said playfully. "You can't tell a New Yawk accent when ya hears one?"

"No way. You're from New York?"

"Yeah," Dina said with a laugh, "but it's not that exciting."

They passed the ball back and forth for a few minutes without talking, since Coach Matthews was wandering nearby. Christine bumped it a little too hard, and Dina chased it down.

"You there," Coach Matthews called to Christine, "use your legs. Don't just swing your arms." She bent her legs to show Christine what to do.

Dina tossed the ball, and Christine successfully bumped it back. Coach Matthews nodded her satisfaction.

Dina passed the ball to Christine.

"Good job, Stretch," Coach Matthews said and then headed to another pair of girls.

As soon as the coach was out of earshot, Christine started giggling. "She called you Stretch."

"Yeah, I heard." Dina didn't have time to think about it because Coach Matthews changed the drill to setting. They spent a few hectic minutes setting and then moved on to flat-footed kills and digs.

"Laps," Coach Matthews barked when they finished the kill-and-dig drill.

Dina stood in line behind Christine at one of the two water fountains. She was still a little breathless after what seemed like six hundred laps. "Hey, Christine, did ya play on yer sixth grade team he-uh?" Dina laughed. "heeeere. Did you play here?" She groaned in frustration. *Not* speaking New Yorkese was hard.

"Uh huh. Did you play at your school last year?"

"Yeah." Dina took a long drink and then another quick one. "I played on a club team, too. The Hawkinsville Honeys."

Christine laughed.

"I know. Seriously," Dina said. "We all hated that name. We wanted tuh be the Hawkinsville Hornets or somethin' cool, but our coach wouldn't change it."

"I want to try out for a club team this year," Christine said. "The West Lafayette Landsharks. They travel all over. They even went to Chicago last year."

"They did?" Dina had never been to Chicago.

"Yeah, but you have to be invited to try out. And I won't get invited, like, ever."

Dina opened her mouth to reassure Christine, but Coach Matthews started counting down. They hustled back to the court. If all the girls weren't back on the court by the time she got to zero, they'd have to redo all those laps.

"Ten . . . nine . . . eight," Coach Matthews continued.

Dina groaned. Two of the girls apparently didn't hear the countdown or maybe just didn't care, because they sauntered their way back to the court.

"Thanks to Brittany Nelson and Marguerite Dunlop you now have five more minutes of laps," Coach Matthews said way too calmly. "Go." She pointed to their starting point.

"Drill sergeant," Dina mumbled under her breath. Actually, she was more upset at the girls named Brittany and Marguerite than at her new coach.

On her first lap around the court, she looked up at her mother in the stands. As promised, her mother smiled and threw her a thumbs up. Dina waved back as she ran.

"Faster," Sergeant Matthews yelled. "And don't cut corners."

Dina groaned as she picked up the pace. She wasn't sure how much more of this corn country boot camp she could take.

Chapter 2
Boot Camp—Day Two

Dina grabbed her volleyball bag and headed toward the garage door just off the laundry room. "Mom, are you ready yet? I can't be late to tryouts."

"Coming, honey." Her mother adjusted her silk scarf in the mirror in the front hall. She grabbed her briefcase and ushered Dina out the door and into the garage. "How many days of these tryouts left?"

"Just today and den Monday. We get Saturday and Sunday awf."

"Off."

"What?" Dina tossed her bag into the backseat and plopped in the front passenger seat. She buckled her seatbelt.

"Try to pronounce your words less, uh, New York."

"Okay, I'll try, but it's hawd." Dina groaned. "Harrrd. It's hard to speak prop-er-ly." She over enunciated every word and then grinned at her mother, quite pleased with herself.

"That's a good start." Her mother hit the garage door opener and backed the Crown Victoria out of the driveway. "School starts Tuesday, right?"

"Yeah. How come school starts in August he-uh? I mean, heeere. Robyn still has two weeks of summuh vacation left." Robyn Goodman was her best friend at home on Long Island.

"Somebody owes you two weeks of summer, don't they?"

"Seriously." Dina laughed.

"Have you talked to Robyn recently?"

"Yeah. She's goin' to that elite volleyball camp at Suffolk Community College this week." Dina hoped her mother hadn't heard the disappointment in her voice. Going to camp with Robyn had been the only thing she'd wanted to do that summer.

"Oh, honey, I know you miss home, but you'll make a lot of

new friends here. And we can always fly Robyn out here to visit any time."

"I know, Mom." She looked out the window at miles and miles of green plants going by. Maybe those were the soybeans. "I just miss home is all."

"When are they posting the team lists?"

"Tuesday mornin' outside the P.E. teachers' awe . . ." Dina heard her New York accent, " . . . office." She sighed. Living in corn country was tiring.

"From what I saw, you'll make that team no problem. Hey, let's call Daddy tonight and tell him how well you're doing."

"Okay." Dina perked up. Her father's many business trips often kept him away from home for weeks at a time. "When's he comin' home?"

"He wanted to get home before school started, but he can't wrap up his meetings in Kuwait by then."

Dina missed her dad when he went away on business, but she was used to it. The company he worked for, Nammurg Corporation, was a global defense and technology company that sent him all over the world. He had to check in at the New York home office every now and then, but other than that, he pretty much worked from home when he wasn't travelling.

They pulled up to the gymnasium at Earhart Middle School, and Dina sat in the car for a minute before getting out.

"Are you okay, honey?" her mother asked.

"Tryouts are just—" Dina sighed. "I dunno. Tryouts are seriously nerve wracking."

She loved volleyball, but she didn't have any friends at this new school, except maybe Christine now, and she wasn't looking forward to another one of Sergeant Matthews's tryout days. After the extra set of laps at the call out practice the night before, they had worked on serves, did pushups, worked on setting for outside hitters, did sit-ups, and ended the hour-and-a-half workout running more laps. The practice looming ahead of her was scheduled for three whole hours with the added bonus of no parents in the stands.

"Oh, you'll be fine. Now, go get 'em. I'll pick you up at eleven, okay?"

"Okay."

"Do you have your cell phone in case you get out early?"

"Yeah." Dina kissed her mom goodbye and got out of the car. She steeled herself for another day at boot camp.

Brittany Nelson and Marguerite Dunlop pulled up in a car right behind hers. Brittany stepped out of the car and put her bag down. She pulled her long blonde hair into a pony tail. Marguerite pushed her silver wire-rimmed glasses up the bridge of her nose and stood behind Brittany, her bag slung over her shoulder.

"Hey, you're Dina, right?" Brittany smoothed down her ponytail and fell into step with Dina. Marguerite remained a step behind them.

Dina nodded. "And you're Brittany, right?" She opened the door to the gym and let Brittany go through first.

Marguerite hesitated for a second when Dina held the door open for her to pass through.

Dina stuck out her hand. "I'm Dina Jacobs."

"Hi." Marguerite seemed surprised that Dina had actually spoken to her. They shook hands. "I'm Marguerite Dunlop, and you're, like, totally awesome."

"Oh, thanks." Dina felt her cheeks get hot. "I'm seriously sore from yestidday. How 'bout you?"

"I know, I'm so—"

"Anyway." Brittany maneuvered in between them and steered Dina toward the gym. "So where are you from? Boston or something?"

"New Yawk. Longuyland."

"Where's Longuyland?"

"Long I-land," Dina enunciated.

"Oh. Why didn't you say so?" Brittany linked arms with Dina and steered her toward the bleachers. Marguerite trailed behind. "Our sixth grade team was pretty good last year, but we could use a tall player like you."

"I hope I make the team."

"Phht. You will. Don't you just *love* Coach Matthews?" Brittany rolled her eyes. "Criminy, she thinks she knows everything."

Before Dina could come up with a response, Christine saved the day by bursting into the gym. "Am I late?"

Dina laughed. "No, I think we're a little bit early. I don't even see Coach Matthews."

"Oh, thank goodness. I overslept." Christine sat on the gym floor, opened her bag, and dumped everything out. She grabbed her sneakers and a hair tie and then shoved the extra pair of socks, shorts, t-shirt, wallet, gum, and a set of keys back in.

Dina chuckled.

"What?" Christine asked with a grin.

"Nuttin'. I just never saw anybody do that." Dina opened her own gym bag and gently took out her sneakers. She put them on and then pulled her jet black hair back into her usual tacked-up ponytail. She smiled when Christine did the same to her light brown hair.

"So, Dina," Brittany said. "Did you play on your sixth grade team on Long Island?"

"Yeah. Wait. No."

"Which is it?" Brittany exchanged a glance with Marguerite.

"We didn't have a sixth grade team. We just had one middle school team. I guess volleyball isn't as popular on Longuyland, I mean Long Island. Suffolk Community College has a team, but—"

"I want to play for Penn State," Marguerite blurted.

"Penn State?" Brittany said with disbelief. "They stink."

"Uh, no, they don't, Brittany," Christine said. "Not only were they the Big Ten champs two years in a row, but they were the NCAA champs back to back, too."

"Whatev," Brittany said with derision. "If you want to go anywhere in volleyball, you have to play for a California team."

"Like who?" Christine challenged.

"Criminy. C'mon, people. You have to play for Stanford, girls. That's the ticket for getting to the Olympics. Logan Tom and Ogonna Nnamani played for Stanford. Kerri Walsh, too. Please tell me you all know she and Misty May won the beach volleyball gold medal at the last Olympics."

"Hey," Christine said, "did you guys watch indoor volleyball in the Olympics last summer?"

"No," Dina admitted a little too quickly.

Brittany and Marguerite stared at her in astonishment.

"What?" Dina shrugged. "We were on a . . . We were on vacation."

She almost said that she and her family were on a cruise around the Hawaiian Islands, but she wasn't sure if people from Indiana went on cruises. She also felt kind of stupid that she hadn't watched the Olympic volleyball games. She and Robyn had never watched volleyball on TV. Maybe she was right when she'd told her mother that the kids in Indiana played volleyball 24-7. "How did Team USA do?"

Brittany started to answer, but Christine shushed her. "Don't tell her. I have all the games recorded on DVD's, and she can watch them for herself."

"What countries played in the—?" Dina started.

"Team USA was in Group A with Japan, China, Venezuela, Poland, and Cuba," Marguerite said.

"And group B was Brazil, Italy, Russia, Serbia, Kazakhstan, and and and . . . Shoot, there was one more." Brittany stomped her foot.

"Algeria," Marguerite finished smugly.

"Ah," Brittany groaned. "You're such a brainiac. Team USA wasn't ranked very high, so nobody predicted a medal for them."

"Seriously? Did we get one?"

"You really don't know what happened?" Christine raised an eyebrow.

Dina shook her head and felt really stupid in front of her new friends.

"Okay, for real. Nobody tell her." Christine glared at Brittany and Marguerite.

They nodded, and then Brittany tapped Marguerite on the arm. "C'mon, brainiac, I have to practice my sets."

"Okay." Marguerite got up with a grunt and lumbered behind Brittany.

"Do you want to come over tomorrow and watch one of the Olympic games at my house?" Christine asked. "We can watch Team USA play Japan."

"Cool." Dina instantly felt better. Nobody would ever replace her best friend Robyn, but it would be fun to hang out with Christine. "I just have to ask my mom is all." They stood up and walked to the unlocked bin of volleyballs, and Dina took one out. "Oh wait, I have to go to Temple tomorruh mornin', but after that, I'm sure I can come ovuh."

"We really have to work on that accent of yours. Is there a shortage of r's in New York or something?" Christine laughed.

Dina felt her cheeks get warm. "My mom is always pesterin' me about my accent." She sighed. "Okay, fine. I'll try to pronounce things prop-er-ly, but if I don't, help me out, okay?"

Christine nodded. "Deal. Now what did you mean when you said you had to go to Temple? The Taj Mahal kind of temple?"

Dina laughed. "I don't think the Taj Mahal is a temple. It's a tomb for some Indian queen or somethin'."

"It is?"

"Yeah, I'm going to go there someday."

"Me, too."

"I go to Temple Beth Israel for services on Satuhday," Dina said as they stretched. "I'm Jewish."

"Really?" Christine said. "I never met anybody who was Jewish."

"You probably know some Jewish people, but don't realize it."

Christine seemed to think about it for a second. "Yeah, you're probably right, and you know what?"

"What?" Dina bumped the ball to Christine to start their warm up.

"My grandma always said, 'Variety is the spice of life.' I'm Catholic, by the way."

"That's cool. I agree with your Grandma."

Dina opened her mouth to ask what time Christine wanted her to come over the next day, but Coach Matthews barked for attention.

"Balls away," Coach Matthews ordered. "Warm up laps. Five minutes."

Dina groaned and threw the ball in the bin and started her second day of boot camp.

Chapter 3

Team USA vs. Japan

Dina stretched before sitting on the couch in Christine's living room. "I can't believe how sore I am after only two days of tryouts."

"I'm sore, too. It's all those pushups." Christine turned the television on with the remote control. She picked up a second remote and turned on the DVD player.

Dina raised an eyebrow. "How many remotes do ya need?"

"Oh, we've got a lot more." Christine pointed at the television console, and Dina laughed at four more remotes lined up in a row.

"That's crazy."

"What's crazy?" Christine's mother asked as she came in the living room, car keys in hand.

Dina saw the resemblance between mother and daughter immediately. They both had light brown hair, brown eyes, and the same button nose. She tried not to be self-conscious about her own nose, because she thought it was too honkin' big.

"Dina wanted to know why we have three thousand remotes."

Christine's mother laughed.

"Oh, sorry, Mom. This is Dina. My new friend I told you about."

Dina stood up and shook Christine's mother's hand. "It's nice to meet 'cha, Mrs. Hannigan. Thanks for letting me come ovuh to watch the game. My mom told me to tell you she's sorry she couldn't come in to meet 'cha, but she was already kinda late for her office hours."

"No problem. I'm sure I'll meet your parents soon enough. At a volleyball game, I imagine."

Dina nodded. "Yeah, my mom usually comes to every game."

"Thanks for helping Christine babysit this afternoon."

Dina shot Christine a look.

Christine smiled sheepishly. "Oh, did I forget to mention we're watching my four-year-old brother, Joey, while Mom goes to pottery?"

As if on cue, Joey came tearing through the living room wearing his Batman pajamas and clutching a blue towel around his neck. The towel billowed out behind him as he flew around the room.

"Joey," Mrs. Hannigan said, "I told you to get out of those pajamas."

Joey continued to run circles around the couch. Dina pulled her legs up so the pint-size superhero wouldn't collide with her.

"I'm outta here." Mrs. Hannigan laughed. "Good luck, honey."

Christine stuck her tongue out at her mother, but Dina could tell it was in fun. "Thanks a lot, Mom. I hope your clay melts."

"Good one. Daddy will be home from the plant about the same time I will. Call me if you need me."

"Okay, Mom," Christine called after her mother.

Christine and Dina finally got Joey calmed down with a combination of orange Hi-C in a sippy cup and a bucketful of Duplo Legos. Christine pressed *play* on the DVD player, and the NBC broadcast came to life.

"Oh, no," she cried.

"What's wrong?"

"I forgot. The DVR messed up last summer, and we didn't get the whole match. The first three sets are missing."

"Oh, no." Dina frowned, but didn't know what to do to help.

"Shoot." Christine sighed. "I'm sorry. We'll just have to watch the game from the fourth set on."

"That's okay. I don't care. Hey, look. At least we're winnin' two sets to one. It's best three outta five, right?" She cringed inside. She had seriously been trying to keep her New York accent in check, but when she was excited, nervous, or tired it took on a life of its own. And, to be honest, she was both excited and a little nervous visiting her new friend's house.

"Yeah," Christine said, "if Team USA wins this set, they would win their first match of these Olympics."

"Did they?"

"I'm not telling." Christine grinned. She twisted an imaginary key over her lips and tossed it behind her. "It doesn't look good, though, 'cuz we're already losing this game five to four."

Dina took a sip of her orange Hi-C. "I don't know who any of our players are. I feel kind—" She caught herself from saying, "kinda." She cleared her throat. "I feel kind of stupid not knowing any of them."

Christine laughed. "I don't know them all either, but see number six? The girl with the long, blond braid? That's Nicole Davis, my favorite player. Obviously, she's the libero."

"Yeah, the different colored uniform gives that away." Dina grinned. "I could never be a libero."

"Why not? That's what I want to play."

"Liberos are defensive specialists. They never get to play the front row." That would be the worst thing ever in Dina's world.

"So we don't get the big kills, but teams need us little guys, too." Christine beamed and sat up taller. "I'm only five foot two."

"Okay, that's a good reason. At five nine, I guess I'd make a pretty bad libero."

Christine laughed, and pointed at the television screen. "Oh, hey, there's Logan Tom."

"Who's Logan Tom?"

"You don't know who Logan Tom is?"

Dina shook her head.

"Number fifteen. She's only the best outside hitter, like, ever."

"Really? Which one is she again?"

Christine pointed. "The girl with the really dark hair like yours."

"Okay, I see her," Dina said. "I like their uniforms."

"Yeah, they're cool. Blue and red spandex."

"Do we have to wear spandex?"

"Nah. The eighth grade team does, but we wear regular shorts. If we make the team, that is."

"Oh, right. We can't count our chickens before they're hatched, right?"

"Exactly. Joey, no!" Christine grabbed Joey's hand before he put another Lego block into her glass of Hi-C. She fished out the first Lego and wiped it with a tissue. "Go fly somewhere, Batman."

"No!" Joey sat on the floor with a thump.

"Fine, sit there. Batman doesn't fly anyway." Christine rolled her eyes at Dina.

Dina chuckled and then looked back at the television. Logan Tom dove and rolled for a ball. Unfortunately, she missed, and the point went to Japan.

"That was cool," Dina said.

"What was? I didn't see. I was watching the bat-freak over there." Christine nodded toward Joey.

Dina pointed at the replay on the screen. "Tom. She did an awesome roll. I can't roll like that. We learned how to dive forwuhd last year, but that was about it. Even then, none of us evuh dove in a game."

"We learned to dive forward and to roll to each side last year. I dove a few times, but I'm a lot closer to the ground than you are."

"Seriously."

Dina's mouth fell open when Logan Tom leaped high above the net and sent a nuclear missile crashing down onto Japan's side of the court. She gave Christine a wide-eyed look. "I want to be Logan Tom. I'm glad she plays for our country."

"You're star struck. Tom reminds me of you actually."

"Me? No way. I wish I could leap like that, but I'm not that strong, eithuh."

"Someday we'll both be Olympic strong, right?"

Dina nodded, but wasn't so sure she'd ever be that good. She watched Tom take the ball behind the end line to serve. Tom threw the ball high in the air, took three power steps, and leaped for a jump serve. "I want to learn howta jump serve like that."

"It's not easy."

"Darn," Dina yelled when Japan scored the point on Tom's serve. "I can't believe we're still losing this game. Has Japan evuh won the gold medal?"

"Yeah, I think they won twice, but the last time was a really long time ago, like in 1976 or something."

"Who won in 2004?"

"China, but they weren't the favorite that year."

"Who was?" Dina glanced at Christine.

"Brazil, I think."

"Cool. A South American team."

"Oh." Christine cringed when a Japanese player blocked a Tom hit. "Nice block. This Japan team looks pretty good, don't they?"

"Yeah, they do. Ooh, time-out. Good. We need one right about now."

The camera zoomed in on Team USA's Coach Lang Ping giving instructions to her players.

"So,uh, have *we* evuh won the gold?"

"Have we everrrrrrr won the gold? Your devious attempt to reveal the outcome will not work, *Stretch.*"

Dina laughed. "Hey, I tried."

Christine glanced at her brother. He placed another Lego brick on the top of his ever-growing skyscraper. "Well, actually, before these Olympics, I think we won a silver and a bronze, but that was way before we were born. We were supposed to win the gold in 1980, though."

"But we didn't?"

"Nope." Christine shook her head. "We didn't get to play."

"How come?" Dina couldn't imagine why Team USA wouldn't get to play in the Olympics. "Did they all get sick or somethin'?"

"No, the Olympics were in the Soviet Union that year, and the president said we had to boycott, so nobody from the USA went that year."

"Nobody?"

"Nope."

Dina couldn't believe that a president would take away so many people's dreams. "That stinks. Which president?"

"Jimmy Carter. My mom said he pulled us out of the Olympics because the Soviet Union was in a bad war with Afghanistan or something. A whole lot of other countries boycotted, too, so we weren't the only one."

"Wow. I feel bad for all those athletes."

"I know, me too. Especially because our volleyball team was ranked first going into the Olympics. Last year, Team USA was only ranked fourth."

"So they're not expected to get any kinda medal then?"

Christine shook her head.

"Team USA," the Olympic team yelled as their time-out ended. They scampered back onto the court.

Dina gestured toward the screen. "Do you think we'll evuh be good enough?"

"To play in the Olympics?" Christine raised both eyebrows and shrugged. "Ya think?"

"Why not?" Dina said.

"Let's do it."

"Okay." Dina did a few quick calculations in her head. "2020 Olympics. See ya there."

"Okay, 2020. It's a deal." They shook hands.

They watched the game in relative quiet, interrupted occasionally by Joey destroying his Lego structures and rebuilding. They watched play after play, and Dina couldn't take her eyes off the screen. She was amazed at the strength and talent of not only the Team USA players, but the Japanese players as well.

"Do ya hear the crowd?" Dina said as Team USA ran back onto the court after another time-out.

"USA! USA! USA! That must be amazing to hear when you're playing. No one at Earhart Middle ever chanted for us last year. Can you imagine? Earhart! Earhart! Earhart!"

"Seriously." Dina laughed. Logan Tom leaped high above the net and blocked a Japan hit. "Oh, yeah." She pumped a fist. "Nice block, Tom," she yelled at the television screen. "She skied about twelve feet above the net for that one. Hey, what's the score now? I wish they'd keep it on the stupid screen the whole time."

"There it is." Christine pointed. "We're winning twenty-three to twenty-one."

Team USA served the ball over the net. A hitting error by a back row Japanese attacker made the score twenty-four to twenty-one in Team USA's favor.

"One more and we win," Christine said. "Who's serving?"

"Number eleven. Who's that?"

"Robin Ah Mow-Santos." Christine sat up tall and scooted to the edge of the couch. Dina did the same.

"C'mon Santos!" Dina yelled.

Santos's floater serve went up and over the net. A back row Japanese player got under the ball and passed it offline to her setter. The setter somehow dug the ball up for the attack. Dina held her breath as the outside hitter pulled back and smashed the ball toward Team USA. Two USA blockers jumped. The ball ricocheted off their outstretched hands and hit the floor on Japan's side of the court. Match USA.

Dina and Christine leaped up off the couch.

"We did it," Dina yelled and linked arms with Christine. They doe-se-doed around the living room. Joey leaped up and ran circles around them, his Batman cape streaming behind.

"Who says we can't win a gold medal now?" Dina sat back down on the couch, but then remembered the game was a year old.

"Ah, who knows?" Christine sat down with a grin. "Now promise me you won't go Googling to see who won."

Dina put up her right hand and crossed her heart with her

left. "I promise." She bumped fists with her new friend from Indiana.

The Lego tower came crashing to the floor, and Christine rolled her eyes. "Do you want to watch Team USA play Cuba next?"

Dina's smile was instant. "Yeah, yeah. I'm hooked."

Chapter 4
The First Day of School

Dina couldn't believe her luck. She and Christine were in the same first period social studies class together. Maybe the first day of school wouldn't be so bad after all. She sat behind Christine in the row near the windows.

"That was an awesome game against Japan, wasn't it?" Christine asked.

"Yeah, but I can't believe we didn't win one stinkin' set against Cuba." Dina smacked her desk with an open palm.

"I know, but Cuba was ranked pretty high, like, third in the world."

"Yeah, but you said we were ranked fourth. Right behind them."

"We were."

"Brittany said Team USA wasn't supposed to get a medal at all."

"Nope." Christine grinned.

"Oh, c'mon. You're not gonna tell me, are ya?"

"Nope."

Dina scrunched up her nose. "You are so mean." She smiled to let Christine know she was kidding.

Christine grinned back.

"Hey," Dina pulled a brand new notebook out of her book bag, "that number fifteen? Logan Tom? She has mad skills."

"I know. She made about a thousand kills in each match. And my Nicole Davis was awesome, too." Christine pulled out her own brand new notebook.

Dina gasped. "I didn't have time to check the volleyball list this morning. Did we make the team?"

Christine clamped her lips tight.

"C'mon. Did we make it? I can't check until lunchtime."

Dina couldn't tell if Christine was hiding a smile or not. She didn't know her well enough to be able to tell.

Christine held her lips tight, but pointed to herself and nodded.

"You made the team?"

Christine nodded again, obviously trying to hide a smile.

"C'mon, did *I* make it, too?" Dina pointed toward herself.

Christine shrugged and looked up at the ceiling as if she had no idea.

"Oh, c'mon. Don't tor-chuh me."

Christine returned her gaze to Dina and grinned. "So, uh, what are you doing this afternoon? Say around three-thirty?"

"I dunno," Dina said, bugging her eyes out. "Do you think I could be goin' to volleyball practice?"

Christine shrugged again and tried to keep a straight face, but couldn't. "Yes, of course you are. We both made the team."

Dina wanted to ask who else had made the team, but the bell rang to start the class. Their new social studies teacher, Mr. Robertson, cleared his throat for attention. Christine turned toward the front of the room.

"Vel-come," Mr. Robertson rumbled in a deep eerie Halloween voice. "You have entered the Social Studies Zone. Mwu-ha-ha-ha."

Dina giggled. Mr. Robertson was going to be fun. He wore dark blue jeans with a long-sleeved red, white, and blue striped shirt. His mustache and beard were gray, almost white, and the beard hid his double-chin. Kind of. His eyes were almost completely hidden behind his thick black-rimmed glasses, but Dina could see the mirth in them. She breathed a sigh of relief. Thank goodness everyone in Indiana wasn't as strict and serious as Coach Matthews.

Dina stretched her sore back muscles and opened her notebook to the first page.

Mr. Robertson handed out the seventh grade social studies course outline. Dina was excited to see that they were going to study non-western countries. She hoped they could learn about places like the Taj Mahal in India and the Pyramids in Egypt and the Great Wall of China. Her father had been to all of those places, and someday she hoped to go there, too. He still wasn't home from his trip yet. He said he had to stay in Kuwait to "smooth some feathers."

Mr. Robertson leaned forward on his lectern. "And now comes the grim part of the course," he said with his evil laugh. "The class rules."

The twenty-five seventh graders groaned in unison.

"That's exactly the kind of thing I'm talking about." Mr. Robertson poked the air at them. At first Dina thought he was mad, but then she saw the gleam in his eye. "Even if you don't like something, you must always remain respectful." The class became quiet as he looked them over. "Your groaning indicated to me, quite loudly I might add, that you're less-than-enthused about rules." He made air-quotes when he said the word rules. "But in order for us to work together effectively, we need some guidelines. Mine are easy. There are only two. One—be nice. And two—work hard."

Dina chuckled softly along with her classmates. These seemed like pretty easy rules to live by.

Mr. Robertson laughed with them, and Dina could tell that he didn't really like the role of disciplinarian. "Okay, you guys. Enough of that. Turn to the third page of the course outline."

Dina turned to the page and found a list of projects they would be doing throughout the year.

"Do you see the second bullet point?" Mr. Robertson paced from one end of the room to the other.

Dina read the second bullet point. Oh, yeah, Mr. Robertson's class was going to be a lot of fun.

Mr. Robertson nodded. "Yep. We're bringing back Show-and-Tell. Every Friday, one of you will bring something to the class that'll help the rest of us become more informed about the world. Now since we'll be focusing on the non-western world, I encourage you to bring in something that spotlights those parts of the world, but, really, anything goes for Show-and-Tell. Just keep it clean and appropriate for school." He wagged his finger at the class. "Remember that 'be nice' clause?"

Dina already knew what she was going to bring in for Show-and-Tell. She had a collection of coins that her dad brought her from all over the world. She had coins from Spain, China, Japan, India, Syria, and even Israel. She definitely wanted to show the class some of the new shekels she had. She bet Mr. Robertson would think they were cool.

Mr. Robertson walked to the overhead projector and turned it on. A map of Asia displayed on the screen. "Let me give you an example of what I mean by Show-and-Tell, and I don't mean the map." He picked up something from his desk and clenched it in his fist. "Yesterday, when I was getting my act together for school today, I turned on the overhead and kaplooie! The bulb popped." He laughed. "It was really quite spectacular. You guys should have been here."

Christine turned around and rolled her eyes at Dina as they laughed.

"Anyway," Mr. Robertson continued, "I scurried over to the cabinet and pulled out a new bulb." He opened his palm and showed the class a tiny overhead bulb. Dina was amazed at how small it was. "This is the *show* part. I'm showing you something, and now I have to *tell* you about it. What's so special about this light bulb? How can this light bulb have world ramifications? Where do you think this bulb was made?"

A few classmates raised their hands and suggested countries like Japan, China, and India. Mr. Robertson shook his head at each one.

Christine raised her hand. "The USA?"

"Another good guess, but no." He pointed toward the map on the screen. "The answer is on that map." He picked up a small laser pointer from his lectern and pointed. "The overhead bulb that is currently shining this map was made in Vietnam."

Dina was surprised. The only time she'd ever heard about Vietnam was when people talked about the war and POW's and such. Mr. Robertson explained that Vietnam was becoming a technological country and had even developed an institute for space technology.

Dina was surprised when the bell rang to end class. It seemed like they had just gotten started. She put her notebook and pen back in her book bag. She was amazed at how much she had learned in the first period of the very first day of school. She had gotten so involved with Mr. Robertson's discussion of Vietnam that she had almost forgotten that she had made the volleyball team. Almost.

She tapped Christine on the shoulder as she stood up. "I'm so psyched we both made the team."

"I know. We're awesome." Christine leaped up out of her chair and hugged Dina. They jumped up and down.

"I have to call my mom, but I can't. I have to go to math. Which way's math?" Dina grabbed her backpack and pulled it over both shoulders.

Christine linked arms with Dina, and they hurried out of Mr. Robertson's Social Studies Zone. She pointed down the hall in the direction of Dina's math classroom.

"See ya at practice later," Dina called after Christine who headed the other way.

Christine turned around and threw Dina two thumbs up.

Chapter 5
Stretch

"Okay, girls," Coach Matthews said, "bring it in here."

Dina ran onto the court and joined Marguerite and a few of the other girls. They were going to practice approaching the net for hits. Christine and Brittany, meanwhile, were on the other side of the net with the rest of the team, practicing digs and sets.

Dina looked around. At five foot nine, she was the tallest one in the gym, except for Coach Matthews who was taller than everybody. Dina was even taller than Coach Vaughn, the eighth grade coach.

"First let's practice the arm swing. Keep your arm loose, don't stiffen up."

Dina wiggled her right arm to make sure it was loose.

"Okay," Coach Matthews continued, "swing both arms behind you and then up. Like this." She demonstrated the arm swing. "Did you see how my left hand points toward the imaginary ball and my right arm is bent and ready? It almost looks like you're serving a tennis ball or about to throw a javelin."

Dina nodded. That made a lot of sense. Even though Coach Matthews didn't have a sense of humor, she knew a lot about volleyball. She'd grown up in Indiana, but played volleyball at a college called Northwestern University in Chicago.

"Okay, girls. Let's try just that much."

Dina faced the net and practiced her arm swing.

"Dig deep with those knees, Stretch," Coach Matthews corrected.

"Good job, *Stretch*," Marguerite said with a grin after Coach Matthews had walked on.

Dina smirked, trying hard not to laugh.

"Okay, your power comes from the snap of the wrist," Coach Matthews said. "Bring your right arm through and whip your wrist. Stay loose. Watch me." She demonstrated the movements.

Dina tried to stay loose during the wrist snap. It was kind of hard because she kept imagining slamming the ball down like she'd seen Logan Tom and Tayyiba Haneef-Park do during the Olympic Games. Tayyiba was the tallest player on the team at six-foot-seven inches. Dina wanted to be tall—and probably would be since her father was six foot four and her mother was five ten—but she didn't want to be Tayyiba tall. Maybe Logan Tom tall at six foot one would be good enough. She only had a few more inches to go.

Dina wondered if maybe she'd be good enough to play in the Olympics someday. She'd have to play on a seriously good college team first, though. Maybe Brittany was right, maybe she should go to Stanford or some other college in California.

Coach Matthews added a ball to their drill. "Without jumping, toss the ball high and contact it at its highest point, as high as you can reach."

The girls tried it for a while, and Coach Matthews corrected them by saying things like, "Reach for it. Reach and snap. Good." She watched Dina from behind. "Keep your hitting elbow high. Up by your ear. Now, reach and snap. Yes, yes, yes. Great job, Stretch."

The small adjustments Coach Matthews made felt strange at first, but eventually Dina got the hang of it and smashed the ball with more power than ever.

"You girls are doing great," Coach Matthews said with her arms folded across her chest. "I can't wait to play West Morrill."

Dina couldn't believe their first game was only two weeks away. She looked around at her teammates. She wasn't sure they were going to be ready.

Dina tossed the ball high in the air and smashed it into the floor with the flick of her wrist. It skittered over to Christine's side of the net. Christine picked it up and, with a smile, tossed it back.

Christine went back to her drill. She got low, dove for a ball, and sent it back up to the setter at the net. Dina was impressed. Christine had some seriously mad libero skills going on. Dina was scared about diving. Maybe she'd ask Christine for help.

One thing was for certain, Christine would probably be the starting libero. Brittany seemed to be pretty good as a setter, too. Dina had to stay on Brittany's good side, so she'd get some sets during games.

Coach Matthews told the setters and defensive specialists on Christine's side of the net to clear the floor. She made them do conditioning drills. They started by doing pushups.

Coach added jumping to the hitting drill. She showed them how to approach the net, do a jump stop, swing their arms to propel themselves upward, and channel all their energy into the arm swing and wrist snap. After doing the drill without balls for a few minutes, she paired the players up and had each pair grab a ball from the bin.

"Toss the ball up in front of your partner," Coach Matthews said and tossed a ball high up in front of her. Dina caught it. "Take your jump stop, propel upward, and snap your wrist. Remember to follow through."

Coach motioned for Dina to toss the ball up for her. She took her steps and smashed the ball over the net onto the other court.

"Whoa," Dina said in chorus with the other girls. No wonder Coach made Christine's group move off of the other side of the court.

Marguerite tossed the ball in front of Dina. Dina took her approach and leaped. *Bam!* The ball smashed onto the other side of the court. A lot of the other girls' balls went into the net, but Dina's went over every single time with serious power. She'd learned how to hit on her middle school team in New York, but not like this. The changes Coach Matthews made were awesome.

She slammed the ball over the net several times, and then Marguerite took her turn. Most of Marguerite's slammed smoothly to the other side, but a few got caught in the net.

"Switch again," Coach Matthews commanded.

Dina slammed the ball over the net time and time again. She was lost in the zone, it felt so good. The gym seemed to go quiet, and she glanced around. The rest of her teammates were quietly watching her. She caught Marguerite's next toss instead of hitting it.

Her teammates and Coach Matthews clapped.

Dina wanted to crawl under a rock.

Coach Matthews dismissed them for a short water break and walked over to the eighth grade coach. Christine, Marguerite, and Brittany ran up to Dina.

Christine stared at her. "Who are you and what have you done with Dina?"

"Oh, c'mon." Dina felt herself blush even more.

"You're awesome, Dina," Marguerite said with stars in her eyes.

"Criminy," Brittany added as they walked to the water fountains, "I'm just glad you're on our team."

"C'mon, *Stretch*, let's get some water," Christine teased.

They stopped laughing when Coach Matthews started her countdown.

Chapter 6
Back Home

Dina sat on her bed and rifled through her backpack for her cell phone. She and her mother had just gotten back from Temple, and in about an hour she was going to Christine's house again to watch more Olympic volleyball games. Oh, and they'd be babysitting Joey while Christine's mom went off to her Saturday pottery class. She finally found her cell phone at the bottom, pulled it out, and flopped back against her pillows.

The first week of school had practically flown by, and she had gotten into a nice routine. Every morning her mother dropped her off at school, and Dina went to classes during periods one through four, ate lunch in the school cafeteria during period five with Christine, Brittany, and Marguerite, and then went to classes during periods six through eight. The best part of the day was volleyball practice after school, just like back home.

Back home. Dina had done a lot of thinking about home, recently, and decided she was overdue to call her very best friend in the whole wide world. Robyn wasn't expecting her call, but that didn't matter. They were best friends. Dina didn't need an appointment.

"Hey, Mom?" Dina called out of her open bedroom door.

"Yes, honey?" her mother answered from the kitchen.

"I'm just gonna cawl Robyn before we go, okay?"

"Sure, but not too long. It's long distance now."

"I think I have plenty of minutes."

"All right, go ahead. Oh, and Dina?"

"Yes, Mom?"

"The word is call, not *cawl*."

"Between you and Christine, I'll be speaking proper English any time now."

Her mother laughed. "Tell Robyn I said hello."

"I will." Dina got up and closed the door to her room. She said, "*Schmeggegy*," into her phone, and it dialed Robyn Goodman's phone number. *Schmeggegy* was the Yiddish word that kind of meant dork. Of course, Robyn always said Dina was the dork with her crazy obsession for wanting to travel the world and see exotic places. Robyn thought Dina was nuts for wanting to ride camels in the desert, watch lions in Africa, and snowmobile in Greenland.

The phone rang several times, and then Robyn's voice mail finally picked up. "Hey, why ya callin' me?" Robyn's New York accent made Dina's heart smile. She missed home so much. "You think I got nuttin' bettuh tuh do than tawk to you? Whatevuh. Leave a message." The voice mail beeped.

"Hey, *Schmeggegy*. It's me, your favorite world traveler calling all the way from the cawn capital of the world. I just . . ." Home sickness squeezed her throat closed. She cleared it open and said, "I just called to say, 'hey, boss.' So, what's up? How was volleyball camp? You were supposed tuh call and tell me all about it. How's Rabbi Schwartz?" Dina laughed. "Do people in the front row still have to wear raincoats during service?"

Dina told Robyn's voice mail about the volleyball team and tryouts with Sergeant Matthews. She told her about the classes at Earhart Middle and about the Show-and-Tell in social studies. She was just about to tell her about her new friend Christine, but decided not to. She simply said, "Okay, *Schmeggegy*, I gotta go, I guess. Call me latuh."

She pushed the end button and placed her phone on her bedside stand. Going to the elite volleyball camp at Suffolk Community College together was all they had talked about in sixth grade. She sighed. Her mother seemed to like her new job, but still, it kind of wasn't fair. Nobody asked her whether or not she wanted to leave Long Island.

Now that she'd been away for almost three whole months, she couldn't help the tug at her heart that wanted her to go home. Part of her—no, a lot of her—felt like she and her family had been on an overlong vacation that just wasn't ending.

With a sigh, she got up and went to her closet. She muscled out a heavy safe about a foot square on each side and plopped it on the bed. Her parents had gotten her the safe after she begged and begged for it on her last birthday. She wanted a secure place to keep the international coins her father brought back for her.

She dialed the combination and pulled out her stash of coins. Her goal was to collect coins from every single country in the world. For now her father was her main source, but she wanted to become a famous anthropologist so she could travel and do research. She wasn't sure what kind of research she would do, but she'd figure it out eventually.

On the second day of school, Mr. Robertson had them pull dates out of a hat to determine when they would present their Show-and-Tell projects. She had been kind of unlucky and had pulled the second week of school, so she only had five more days to get her project ready. Some kid was even more unlucky and had to go during the first week. He had brought in his Mizuno baseball glove, and Dina was surprised to learn that Mizuno was a Japanese company that had offices all over the world. She was glad not to be the first one to present, but it was kind of cool to get the whole thing over with early. Christine got an early pick too, and was going in the fourth week.

Dina wanted to bring all her coins in, but knew she wouldn't have enough time, so she decided on Japan, Syria, and Israel. She picked out several coins from each of the three countries and divvied them up into three velvet bags. She stashed the bags into a secret zippered compartment deep inside her backpack, put the remaining coins away, and then returned the safe to the far reaches of her closet.

"Dina," her mother called.

"Yeah?"

"Are you ready to go?"

Dina looked at the clock. *Shoot, it's time to go to Christine's.* "Okay, I'll be there in a minute." She picked up her cell phone. The ringer was on. Maybe Robyn was still at Temple or something and hadn't gotten her message yet. Shoot. What if

Robyn called back while she was at Christine's? She'd have to let it go to voice mail. She couldn't talk on the phone with her best friend from home with her new best friend in Indiana sitting right there. That would be seriously uncool.

Chapter 7
Show-and-Tell

Dina sat in Mr. Robertson's social studies class, clutching her velvet coin bags in a stranglehold. She took several deep breaths and waited for Mr. Robertson to finish going over the quiz they had taken the day before.

Dina leaned close to Christine and whispered, "What time's the game tonight?"

"Purdue plays Ball State at seven," Christine said under her breath. "We'll pick you up for dinner at five o'clock, okay?"

"Cool. I'm glad we have a short practice today."

"Me, too."

"Ready, Dina?" Mr. Robertson asked.

"Yeah."

She headed to the front of the room. Her heart beat faster and faster with every step. Before she got to the front, she took a deep breath and let it out. Her dad had given her that advice over the phone the night before. That's what he said he did when he felt nervous.

She stepped behind Mr. Robertson's lectern, looked out at her classmates, and caught Christine's smile. That made her feel better. For a second.

She cleared her throat. "I have about fifty coins in these three bags. My dad travels all over the world for work and brings me coins. For example . . ." She opened the draw string of the first bag and dumped a few coins onto the lectern. She scattered them and picked up the largest one. "My dad's been to Tokyo, Yokohama, and Osaka. Those are cities in Japan." She shined Mr. Robertson's laser pointer at the cities on the map hanging on the wall. "He says there's this seriously cool aquarium in Osaka he wants to take me to. Anyway, this is a five-hundred-yen coin, and it's worth about five U.S. dolluhs." She groaned inside at the New Yorkese that had slipped out. Her classmates oohed and aahed at the five-hundred-yen coin, which made her relax a little. "I have a couple of 'em that I'll pass around in a few seconds, but on the reverse of this coin you'll see the big five hundred, some bamboo, and Mandarin oranges." She held up the reverse side of the coin to the class even though she knew they couldn't see the detail. She flipped the coin over. "The obverse has the name Japan, in Japanese of course, and some Paulownia flowers."

"Dina," Mr. Robertson interrupted, "why don't you explain the difference between obverse and reverse."

"Oh, okay." She hoped she hadn't lost points. "Obverse means the front and reverse means the back, you know, like, the tails side."

A few of her classmates nodded, and one boy said, "Oh, I get it." That made Dina feel better.

"So what's seriously weird about Japanese coins is that they don't put regular dates on 'em. Like this coin was minted in the year 2007, but the year nineteen is written on it in Japanese. My dad told me it was a nineteen 'cuz he can read some Japanese, but I can't. Not yet. Anyway, the nineteen means that the emperor had been reigning for nineteen years when this coin was made. If we did that in this country, we'd have dates like Obama one and Obama two, I guess. Anyway, Emperor Akihito is the current Japanese emperor, and when he dies, he'll be replaced by his son whose name is Naruhito."

Dina wasn't one hundred percent sure she'd pronounced the names properly, but when she practiced her Show-and-Tell presentation with her dad over the phone the night before, he said she was pretty close.

She held up another Japanese coin. "This one is a ten-yen coin and is just like our dime. And if you haven't figured it out by now, a yen is worth about one U.S. penny. That changes based on the exchange rates, though. This coin has the Hoodo Temple on the obverse and evergreen branches on the reverse. I have a few more coins from Japan in here, but I'll go ahead and pass these around as I talk." She handed the boy in the front row near the windows a handful of her Japanese coins and then walked over to the nerdy girl sitting in the front near the door and handed her the rest.

"Japan has been around a lot longer than the United States, and the Japanese are very proud of their history. You can tell that by all the stuff they jam onto their coins."

Dina talked about her five-yen, fifty-yen, and one hundred-yen coins, but then decided to move on to her coins from Syria. Instead of collecting her Japanese coins, she let them circulate.

"These next coins are from Syria." She pointed to Syria on the world map. "Syria borders Turkey, Iraq, Jordan, Lebanon, and Israel." She held up her last velvet bag. "In fact, this last bag has coins from Israel, but I'll do Syria first." She held up the first Syrian coin. "This one is a twenty-five pound coin and has the Syrian coat of arms on the obverse. The Arabic writing says, 'Syrian Arab Republic.'" Christine raised her eyebrows as if she was impressed that Dina knew Arabic. "Oh, I can't read Arabic." She laughed and turned the coin over. "On the reverse, under the picture of the Central Bank of Syria, it says 'Syrian Arab Republic' in English. It's kinda cool that they have two languages on their coins. I'll pass it around, so you can see." She remembered something her dad had shown her. "Oh, check this. On the reverse, when you tilt it one way you can read the number twenty-five, but when you tilt it back the other way, it reads *CBS* which stands for the Central Bank of Syria." She thought of about a thousand more things to add, but knew she had to watch her time, so she simply added, "This twenty-five pound coin is worth about fifty U.S. cents."

As the students passed the coins from Syria around, she talked about how the twenty-five pound coin was made out of two different colored metals in an attempt to stop counterfeiters. She added that President Hafiz-al Assad had even ordered his own image on the twenty-five pound coin.

The nerdy girl in the front row laughed. "That was kind of a stuck up thing to do."

Dina nodded. She thought so, too.

She didn't have much time left, so she quickly handed out her coins from Israel and said that the new shekel was the current Israeli currency. She told them to notice that the country name, Israel, was written in three languages—English, Hebrew, and Arabic. She started to talk about the lily on the obverse side, when Mr. Robertson pointed toward his watch. She frowned because that meant she had to wrap things up. She felt like she had just gotten started. She loved talking about her coins.

She scanned her brain for some quick, but interesting facts. "Did you know that Israel's coins are minted in South Korea? That's because Israel doesn't have its own mint." She pointed to Israel on the map and then swung the beam to South Korea. "The new shekel is worth about twenty-five U.S. cents, and the new ten shekalim coin is worth about two-dollars-and-fifty cents.

"My parents are gonna take me to Israel next summer with my dad's frequent flyuh miles. If Israel's not at war with Palestine again, that is." She decided not to mention that her parents had given her the trip for her Bat Mitzvah last spring. She kind of got the feeling that her classmates wouldn't understand what a Bat Mitzvah was.

She retrieved her coins from the students in the front row and then jammed them all into one bag. She'd separate them out later.

"Thank you," she said and scurried back to her seat.

"Good job, Dina," Mr. Robertson said, and the class clapped.

Christine swiveled in her seat. "You did great. You'll get an A for sure."

"Phew." Dina blew out a sigh. "I was so nervous."

"You couldn't tell, not really. Your New Yorkese came out a couple of times, though."

"Seriously?" Dina grimaced. She'd been working so hard not to sound different from her classmates.

Mr. Robertson put his hand up for attention. "Dina showed

us coins from three different countries—Japan, Syria, and Israel. Now since we didn't have as much time for Israel, I would like you to research the history of Israel. Let's do our usual. At least one page, handwritten if it's neat, typed if neat is not in your vocabulary." The class laughed. "Oh, and cite your sources. Okay?"

Dina nodded along with her classmates. "That shouldn't be too hard," she whispered to Christine.

"Just don't use Wikipedia." Christine laughed. Using Wikipedia was a big no-no in Mr. Robertson's class, but Dina knew that most of her classmates started their weekly research there.

Mr. Robertson looked at the clock. "Okay, everybody. Go ahead and pack up."

Dina reached down for her backpack.

"Figures the Jew brings in money," a boy with a blonde crew cut said. "My uncle says Jews just love money."

Another boy with curly brown hair laughed.

Dina tightened her fists. She stayed bent over and rooted through her backpack as if she were looking for something. She didn't want to sit back up because she might not be able to control the New York in her which would lay some serious hurt on her two classmates. At least verbally. She released an involuntary groan.

"Don't listen to Aaron," Christine said in a low, angry voice. "He's a jerk."

Dina took a deep breath and said through gritted teeth, "Some people are seriously brain-deficient around he-uh."

"Aaron and Tyler are lowlifes. Just ignore them."

The bell rang. Dina grabbed her backpack and bolted out of her chair. She reached the door at the same time as Aaron and bumped him from behind. She almost smiled at his startled reaction.

She brushed passed and said over her shoulder, "Did you know Aaron is the most popular Jewish name for boys?" She whipped her head back around and stormed into the hallway.

Chapter 8
Triple XXX

Dina sat next to Christine in the farthest backseat of Christine's family minivan. Joey sat buckled up in the seat in front of them, and Mrs. Hannigan drove.

Dina turned to Christine. "Where're we goin' for dinner?"

Mrs. Hannigan glanced back. "Christine figured you'd never been to the Triple XXX, so that's where we're headed."

"Okay," Dina said politely, but was a little confused. Triple XXX? In New York, Triple XXX meant a bad kind of bar where girls didn't wear clothes, not that she had ever been in one, but she couldn't understand why anyone would want to be naked in front of people.

She must have had a worried look on her face because Christine laughed. "Triple XXX is a family restaurant. It's kind of like a New York diner, I think."

"Oh, phew," Dina said with a sigh. "Seriously, I didn't know where you guys were takin' me."

Mrs. Hannigan laughed, and Joey laughed, too, even though Dina was sure he had no idea what they were laughing about.

Dina grinned when they parked next to a cool-looking building with black and orange stripes. There was even an old-timey Coca-Cola sign hanging from the roof. It looked like a fun place to eat.

They sat at a table, and Dina opened her menu.

"Dina," Christine said, "you have to try the Duane Pervis All-American burger."

"Who's Duane Pervis?"

"I don't know. Do you know, Mom?"

"I know he played football for Purdue. In the thirties, I think. He must have been an All-American."

"Duh, Mom." Christine crossed her eyes at her mother.

Dina found the description of the Duane Pervis All-American burger on the menu and chuckled. "Peanut butter? They put peanut butter on a hamburger?"

Christine and her mother laughed, and Joey yelled, "Peanut butter" as loud as he could which set them laughing even harder.

"I don't know about peanut butter, you guys," Dina said. "I think I'll go with the Bernie Flowers All-Pro burger, instead. There's nothin' weird on that one."

"A wise choice." Mrs. Hannigan nodded approvingly.

The waitress came by the table and took their drink orders.

"So, Dina," Mrs. Hannigan said. "Christine tells me you had your Bar Mitzvah this year."

"Oh, no," Dina said. "Bar Mitzvah is for boys. I had my *Bat* Mitzvah in April."

"Oh, so does that mean you're already thirteen?"

"No. Girls have a Bat Mitzvah at twelve. Boys have to be thirteen."

The waitress brought their drinks, and then took their food orders. Dina made sure she ordered her burger without cheese. She and her family weren't super strict about kosher guidelines, but one of the rules they did try to follow was not mixing dairy with meat.

Christine took a quick sip from her Triple XXX root beer. "Why the age difference between girls and boys?"

"Because girls mature soonuh." Dina said the words seriously, but when Christine and her mother laughed, she couldn't help laughing, too.

"So, what exactly is a *Bat* Mitzvah?" Christine asked.

"Bat Mitzvah literally means 'daughter of commandments,' and it means I'm old enough to accept and fulfill G-d's commandments. It's like I'm responsible for my own decisions now, and my parents don't havta take the blame if I do somethin' stupid."

Mrs. Hannigan laughed. "I really like this idea. Christine, let's have a Bat Mitzvah for you right away."

"Ha ha, Mom. You know what, though? A Bat Mitzvah kind of sounds like the confirmation I'm going to make soon."

"It does," her mother said. "So what did you have to do for your Bat Mitzvah?"

"It was a lotta work, actually. I started Hebrew School in fourth grade—"

"I'll have to go to confirmation classes," Christine interrupted.

"Really?" Dina took a sip from her root beer. It was surprisingly good.

"Yeah, once a week I'll go to class and learn about the Bible or something. Right, Mom?"

"Yeah. Oh, Joey, stop that." She took the salt shaker away from him. He had already poured a small pile on the table.

Dina stifled a laugh and composed herself. "On the day of my actual Bat Mitzvah, I was part of the *Shabbat* service and had to recite a lotta scripture in Hebrew. That was kinda hard, especially because the Temple was packed that day. The easy part was the big party we had at the Holiday Inn. A lotta people were there."

"Can I have a big party when I make my confirmation, Mom?"

"Sure, honey. I'm glad to hear you finally getting excited about it."

Christine made a face at her mother, but Dina could tell she was teasing.

"So," Dina asked, "you don't make your confirmation in your church until you're, like, fifteen, right?"

"Yeah, I guess the Catholic Church doesn't think we're ready to be responsible members of society until then."

"You *are* pretty immature."

Christine threw a rolled up straw wrapper at her. Dina ducked.

"No, let me have that." Mrs. Hannigan held her hand out to Joey who put his own balled-up straw wrapper in her palm.

"I guess things are different in our religions," Dina said, "but they're kinda the same, too, you know?"

"Yeah," Christine nodded, "it's kind of like we're all trying to get to the same place, but we get there in different ways."

"Like if we're tryin' to get to the gym for the Purdue volleyball game, and you ride your bike, and I ride a scooter or something. We'll both get there, but differently."

Christine raised an eyebrow. "A scooter?"

"Okay, I've never had a scooter in my life. It was an analogy."

"You can borrow Joey's scooter, anytime," Christine said. "Right, hoosier-boy?"

"Right," he agreed and started playing with his spoon.

"What *is* a hoosier, anyway?" Dina asked.

The waitress appeared with their burgers, and Dina's stomach rumbled. She hadn't realized how hungry she was.

She took a big bite of her Bernie Flowers All-Pro burger minus cheese. "Umm," she said with her mouth full, "this is so good."

Christine and her mother grinned back at her. Dina smiled inside and thought that maybe this weird alien corn-country place wasn't going to be so bad after all.

Chapter 9

Purdue University Boilermakers

Dina and Christine walked into the Purdue University gym behind Christine's mother and brother. Dina couldn't believe hundreds of people were there to watch a college volleyball game. The Suffolk County Community College team never had this many fans.

They followed Mrs. Hannigan into the stands. Dina snuck a peek over her shoulder to watch the Purdue and Ball State teams warm up. She pointed at the Purdue team on the far side of the court. "Spandex shorts. I kind of want to wear spandex next year, but then again, I kind of don't."

Christine laughed. "Yeah, it's like we're on the seventh grade baby team because we still wear shorts and all, but then I don't know if I want to wear something so tight."

"And let all your junk hang out."

"Dina," Christine screeched and started giggling, "you got no junk to hang out, girl."

They found four seats about fifteen rows up across from the Purdue bench. Mrs. Hannigan went in the row first, followed by Joey, Christine, and finally Dina.

Dina laughed at somebody in a weird costume holding an oversized rubber hammer. She nudged Christine and pointed. "What the heck is that?"

"You don't know Purdue Pete? He's a boilermaker. See his hard hat and hammer?"

"What the heck is a boiluhmakuh?" Dina firmly decided that, yes, they definitely did things differently in the Midwest.

"Purdue started out as a school for kids of farmers and factory workers and stuff. They're called working class people or something."

The whistle blew, and the game started.

"So what's a boilermaker?" Dina still couldn't make heads or tails of it. "Someone who makes boilers?"

"Actually, you're pretty close," Mrs. Hannigan said, leaning over Joey. "Boilermakers are people who work on boilers, like the ones in old-fashioned locomotives."

"Oh," Dina said, "I saw that big train on campus. Now I get it."

Mrs. Hannigan nodded. "Purdue didn't come up with its own nickname, though. Back in the day, their football team was pretty good, and newspapers called the Purdue players coal heavers, rail splitters, blacksmiths, boilermakers—any name they could think of that would be insulting."

Dina laughed. "And Purdue chose to call themselves the boilermakers?"

"Apparently."

Dina turned to Christine. "Hey, you never told me what the word hoosier—"

"Look, that's me." Christine pointed at the Purdue team. "Number fourteen. The libero."

"What's her name?"

"That's Blair Bashen. Kelli Miller was last year's libero, and she was really good, but she graduated. I think Bashen red-shirted last year."

"Red-shirted?"

The crowd cheered when a kill by a tall Purdue player wearing number sixteen gave them their first lead by a score of 2-1.

"We're winning." Dina high-fived Christine, and then Joey high-fived everyone, including his mom.

She cheered with the raucous crowd and couldn't help laughing at the seriously loud student section. The college students wore black t-shirts with gold writing and still hadn't sat down. Purdue player number thirteen went up for a kill, and the students held a long yell of, "Ohhhhh," and then punctuated the hit with a crescendo of "Uh!"

Dina quietly echoed the students a few plays later when

Purdue player number sixteen leaped up for another kill. Number sixteen's long brown hair was pulled back into a ponytail. The intense look on her face made Dina glad she didn't have to play against her.

"Who's that?" She pointed at the Purdue circle of players celebrating their latest point.

"That's Kristen Arthurs," Christine said. "She's so awesome. She's their middle hitter."

"Arthurs was the state of Michigan's player of the year in high school," Mrs. Hannigan added.

"Really?" Dina stared at Arthurs wide-eyed. After the first five plays of the first big college volleyball game she had ever seen, she was hooked. Team USA and Logan Tom were still her favorites, of course, but Purdue and Kristen Arthurs were quickly becoming a close second.

Bashen, Purdue's libero, returned a serve.

"So," Dina asked, "what's red-shirting?"

"Oh, yeah," Christine said. "Red-shirting means you practice all year with the team, but don't play in games."

"So Bashen practiced last year, but didn't play?"

Christine nodded. "Umm hmm."

"I'd hate that."

"Me, too."

"Purdue's ranked nineteenth," someone in the stands said.

"Did you hear that?" Dina whispered to Christine.

Ball State's libero served another ball to the Purdue team.

"What?" Christine seemed mesmerized by the game.

"That lady said Purdue was ranked nineteenth."

Christine's jaw dropped. "In the whole country?"

"Yeah."

"Awesome."

They turned their attention back to the game and watched as Ball State scored a point, but then lost the serve on the next play giving Purdue a point.

"Side out," Christine called.

"Side out," Joey mimicked. Christine high-fived him, which

meant that Dina had to high-five him, too, but that was okay. Joey was a cute four-year-old.

Play continued, and Kristen Arthurs flew through the air for another kill.

"Yeah," Dina yelled as Purdue went up by a score of 5-2. "She's got mad skills. Doesn't she?"

"Yeah," Christine agreed, "I think I really want to play volleyball here."

"That would be awesome. You could be the next libero for Purdue. The next Blair Bashen."

"You could be the next Kristen Arthurs or Carrie Gurnell."

"Who's Carrie Gurnell?"

Christine pointed at the Purdue player wearing number thirteen. The tall player leaped high and smashed a kill for another Purdue point. "She's, like, their best outside hitter."

"I wish I was as good as those guys." Dina sat up a little taller. She wasn't sure she wanted to go to Purdue because she hadn't really thought about college, except maybe Stanford, but that was only because of Brittany. Oh, and because Logan Tom had gone there, too. She wondered if Indiana people decided on colleges when they were in middle school. She didn't ever remember talking about college with Robyn. Ever.

Dina turned her attention back to the game. She was mesmerized by the strength and speed of the Purdue players. Kristen Arthurs hadn't missed a kill yet, and Carrie Gurnell was positively scary with the power in her hits. Dina thought she'd hate to be on the other side of the net against either one of them.

A kill from Arthurs made the score 24-19. Dina leaped to her feet and clapped with the rest of the crazy boilermaker fans. On the next play, an attack error by a Ball State player sealed the first set victory for Purdue.

After high-fiving Christine and Joey, Dina sat back down and wondered if Earhart Middle School had a band that played at games like Purdue did. She doubted it. Purdue had cool cheerleaders, too. The guy cheerleaders threw the girls in the air and then caught them in their strong arms. Christine had told her the Earhart cheerleaders only cheered for the football team. That didn't seem fair somehow. Someday, Dina vowed, she would play on a college team with cool cheerleaders and crazy college students and a band that played during timeouts. Someday.

"What's up?" Christine said as the Purdue team served to start the second set. "You have a far-away look on your face."

"Oh." Dina felt herself blush. "No, I just, I was picturin' us playing in college. Like that." She pointed at the court. "It's hard to imagine."

"Yeah, I know. I guess we have to be happy with our little seventh grade volleyball team for now, right?"

"Yeah." Dina cheered at an impressive block by Gurnell and the setter, Tiffany Fisher, at the start of the second set.

"Hey, look." Christine pointed at the court. "That's you and Brittany."

"Yeah, right. I wish I could jump that high."

"I don't think Brittany's going to be very good at blocking, though. You and Marguerite are going to have to do most of it."

"Marguerite's a good middle blocker."

"And you're a good outside blocker, hoosier-girl."

"Hey," Dina said, "if you're gonna call me somethin' at least tell me what it means."

"What? Hoosier?"

"Yeah."

"A hoosier is an Indiana native, so I guess you're not really a hoosier."

"What does it mean, though?"

"I don't know. Some people say it means 'Who's there?' from the old frontier days when people called out of their little cabins and wanted to know who was at the front door."

"That's weird."

"I know. Hey, Mom, what does hoosier mean?"

"Well, it was kind of an insult actually, but most people say it comes from the old English word *hoozer*, h-o-o-z-e-r, which means a large, uncouth person."

Christine frowned. "What's uncouth mean?"

Her mother smiled. "It means a person who doesn't have any manners."

"What?" Christine's jaw fell open. "Mom, wait. You mean Indiana people have no manners?"

Her mother shrugged. "I guess not. Actually, nobody really knows how the word hoosier came about. There are probably a dozen more theories."

Dina nudged Christine. "Hey, hoosier-girl, I can't believe you wanna go to Purdue and add boilermaker to your list of insults."

"Keep a lid on it, New Yawker."

Dina grinned. "Okay, boss."

As the game wore on, Joey squirmed in his seat. He was obviously bored from having to sit still for so long, but he eventually laid his head down in his mom's lap and fell asleep.

Purdue went on to win in straight sets against Ball State for their first victory of the season.

They stood up, made their way down the bleachers with Joey fast asleep in Mrs. Hannigan's arms, and headed out of the gym.

Dina tapped Christine on the arm. "I can't wait to play our first game Tuesday."

"Yeah, West Morrill isn't going to know what hit 'em," Christine said. "Hey, Mom? Can Dina come over tomorrow to watch more Olympic volleyball?"

Dina raised an eyebrow at Christine.

"Is that okay?" Christine asked Dina. "After Temple, of course."

"I have a better idea," Dina said. "Bring the DVDs to my house, and we can have a sleepover."

Christine's face lit up. "Yeah?"

Dina nodded.

"Cool." She turned to her mother. "Can I, Mom?"

"Sure, honey. I'll okay it with Dina's mom when we drop her off. I have to make sure it's okay with her, because I don't like to saddle other people with my children."

"Oh, nice, Mom." Christine made a face at her. Her mother smiled back and shifted the sleeping Joey in her arms.

"All right." Christine linked arms with Dina. They skipped toward the parking lot several yards ahead of Mrs. Hannigan and Joey.

Before moving to Indiana, Dina liked playing volleyball a lot, but after watching Purdue play Ball State and watching the Olympic Games with Christine, she was firmly in love with the sport. Maybe moving to Indiana wasn't so bad after all.

Chapter 10
Logan Tom

Dina put the remote control on the side table and reached for her raspberry-apple Vitamin Water.

"I can't believe you have your own living room," Christine said.

"I don't," Dina protested. "This is the rec room where my dad and I watch TV. No one's allowed in the formal living room 'cept Mom when she watches her shows."

"But you have your own bathroom. I have to share with my little brother."

Dina started to feel a little uncomfortable. She never realized that her new house might be a source of embarrassment. She just thought of it as a house.

"I can't believe you knew all along that Team USA made it to the gold medal game." Dina turned to Christine who was sitting in the recliner. "C'mon. Do they win the gold? Tell me."

"Nope."

"Nope, what? Nope they don't win the gold, or nope you won't tell me?"

Christine turned an imaginary key over her lips and threw it behind her.

"Fine, don't tell me." Dina exaggerated a sigh. "I don't know how we're gonna win, though, because Brazil hasn't lost a game yet. They haven't even lost one single set."

"I know," Christine said. "Can you believe we needed all five sets to beat China?"

"And all five to beat Poland and Italy, too."

"Thank goodness Cuba had the decency to go down in three in the first round of playoffs."

"Seriously." Dina took another sip of her drink and put it on the table. "Ooh, look." She pointed at the television. "There's numbuh fifteen, Logan Tom."

"There's Nicole Davis, too."

Dina's mother tapped on the partially opened door to the rec room. "Are you girls all set for your big game?"

"Yes, Mom. Christine's DVD works fine in our player. We'll probably make popcorn in a little while."

"Oh, good. I'll take some when you do." She pushed a stray lock of hair out of her eyes. Her hair was dark brown, with a few hints of gray throughout. She started to head out the door, but turned back. "Oh, Dina, did you get Christine's sleeping arrangements all set up?"

"Yeah, Mom. I've got both air mattresses on the floor with sleeping bags and pillows."

"Okay, then, I'll be in the back office if you need me. Have fun." She closed the door.

"You're my first sleep ovuh in Indiana," Dina said with a smile.

Christine grinned. "What's a sleep ovuh?"

"Grr," Dina groaned. "Sleep overrr." She stuck her tongue out at Christine, and they both laughed.

"It's much quieter here than at my house."

"Yeah, your brother is cute and all, but . . ."

"I know," Christine said. "Four-year-olds can be a bit much."

"I wanted to invite Marguerite, too, but . . ."

Christine laughed. "But, *criminy*, you'd have to invite Brittany."

They squealed with laughter.

"I used to be really good friends with Brittany, but . . ." Christine shrugged.

"What?"

"She's kind of a fair-weather friend, you know?"

Dina nodded.

Christine looked down for a minute. "Brittany and Marguerite are bff's now, so I was out." Dina opened her mouth to reply, but Christine blurted, "But then you moved here, and you and me can be bff's, okay?"

"Absolutely." Dina couldn't help her widening grin. "Best friends forever." She held her fist out, and Christine bumped it. She pushed *play* on the remote control, and the 2008 Beijing Olympic gold medal volleyball game got started.

A Brazil player hit the ball long.

"Yeah," Dina shouted, "we scored first."

"Do you think that means we're going to win the gold medal?" Christine raised her eyebrows in fake innocence.

"C'mon, tell me."

Christine clamped her lips closed.

"Hoosiers can be so mean. We're gonna get a silver medal at least. I hope we get the gold, though."

Team USA player Kimberly Glass served the ball over the net to the Brazil team.

"Ace," Christine shouted and then leaped out of the recliner.

Dina leaped up, too. They looked at each other, pointed at the sky with their right hand and reached behind them to touch the floor with their left in their point-celebration cheer. They laughed as they sat down.

"I hope we get some aces against West Morrill on Tuesday," Dina said.

"I can't believe our first game is in three days."

"I seriously don't think we're ready."

"Well," Christine said, "maybe West Morrill is as un-ready as we are, right?"

"Ya know, I never thought of it that way. I have hope for us now."

After a few more plays, the Brazil team served the ball to Team USA. The ball went back and forth over the net several times. Neither team seemed to want to give in to the other.

"This is a long volley," Dina said. "Whoa! Did you see Logan Tom dive for that ball? She's so awesome. I wanna be her."

Logan Tom scurried back up to the net and jumped up for a block, but missed the ball.

"Ooh," Christine groaned "You don't want to be Logan Tom now."

"She ate that one, didn't she?" Dina felt bad for Logan.

Several plays later, Tayyiba Haneef-Park served the second ace of the game for Team USA. Dina and Christine did another point-celebration cheer.

A few plays later, Dina leaped to her feet after a spectacularly mad Logan Tom kill. "Did you see that? She went right past both blockers." She sat down in a heap. "That's what I gotta figure out how to do."

"I don't think anybody can block you as it is," Christine said with a grin.

"Yeah, right," she said doubtfully. She felt her cheeks get warm. "Hey, that tied the score seven-seven and, even better, it's a side out."

"I know. I love it when the side out's are in our favor."

"That's way better than side outs that go against you," Dina added.

Logan Tom held the ball in her hand to serve. She threw it high in the air and ran a few steps to time her leap.

"I want to learn how to jump serve like that," Dina said.

Logan's serve hit square into the net, losing the hard-fought side out.

"Oops, maybe not like *that*."

"Maybe Team USA's nervous," Christine offered. "They weren't even supposed to get this far."

"I know." Dina hoped the team would get their nerves under control soon. "Holy!" she yelled at the TV. "Did you see that kill? Who was that?"

"Number seven. Who's number seven?"

"Heather Bown."

"She's a middle blocker," Christine said. "Middle blockers, they're, like, constantly moving. Hitting and blocking. Blocking and hitting. It's tiring to watch."

"Yeah, but Bown's got mad skills like Logan Tom."

"And Dina Jacobs."

"I wish."

With the score tied up 8-8, Heather Bown served the ball

for Team USA. Dina's comparison between Logan Tom and Heather Bown proved to be prophetic as Bown also served the ball into the net for another Team USA service error. Brazil consequently took a one point lead, making the score USA 8, Brazil 9.

"You know," Christine said, "Coach keeps telling us service errors could make or break us."

"Exactly, and it's killin' Team USA right now." Dina gestured toward the television.

Logan Tom tied the score 9-9 with an impressive kill from the back row, and Dina and Christine leaped up and did their point-celebration cheer.

"Tom keeps tying it up," Christine said.

Dina nodded, but she was getting nervous. "I know we still have a long way to go, but we're seriously hangin' with this Brazil team right now."

With the score tied again at 10-10, Logan Tom dove out of bounds to save a ball and then slammed into the scorer's table. Dina cringed, worried that her new favorite player had gotten hurt, but let out a relieved breath as Tom leaped to her feet to rejoin the play. Team USA lost the point, but Dina was positively star struck by Logan Tom.

"I'm going to Stanford," she announced.

"Me, too," Christine agreed, but then laughed. "Except I'm probably going to Purdue."

The game continued, and the score crept up in Brazil's favor. With Team USA down by a score of 11-16, their libero, Nicole Davis, dove for a ball with one arm. The ball popped back up into play.

"What a dig." Christine was obviously as star struck as Dina. "She's always on the floor."

"Just like you."

Despite the extraordinary effort by Team USA, Brazil out-muscled them and won the first set by a score of 15-25.

"Bummer," Dina said. "C'mon, let's go make popcorn. I'll put the second set on pause."

Christine sighed. "Yeah, I think we need cheering up."

They went into the center of the house to the large kitchen, and Dina became self-conscious about all the brand new appliances. She hoped Christine didn't feel weird being in her house. She cleared her throat to hide her nervousness and pulled out two bags of microwave popcorn from the walk-in pantry.

"Hey," Christine said, "is Dina short for something?"

"Yeah." Dina put one of the two bags into the microwave. "Adina. It means 'gentle' in Hebrew."

"Which you are. Except on the volleyball court. You're pretty fierce there."

"Thanks. I think." Dina punched the numbers on the microwave and hit the *start* button.

"Are you, like, named after your grandmother or something?" Christine settled on one of the kitchen stools and set her chin on her fists.

"Oh, no. It's really bad luck to give a baby the same name as a living relative."

"How come?"

"Well, they say if two people have the same name, the angel of death might not be able to figure out who to take. You know, he might mix up who's who and take the new baby to heaven instead of the other relative."

"Uh, oh," Christine said with a worried look on her face.

"What's the matter?"

"I'm named after my aunt."

"Oh, don't worry." Dina took the fully popped bag out of the microwave and put the second one in. She went to the cupboard and got out three small bowls. "I'm sure you'll be just fine."

"Pinky swear?"

Dina laughed. "Pinky swear? I haven't done that since second grade." She linked pinkies for a moment with Christine. The second bag finished popping, and Dina took it out of the microwave. She poured an equal amount into each bowl. "C'mon, let's bring one of these bowls to my mom and then get back to the game and kick some Brazilian butt."

Chapter 11
Merry Kwanukahmas

"Do you want another Vitamin Water or somethin'?" Dina asked.

Christine held up her half-empty bottle. "Nope, I'm good."

Team USA scored the first point in the second set of the gold medal game, and they clapped and cheered.

"Wait," Dina said. "The last time we scored first, we lost."

"Ah, but it's side out, and we get the serve, so maybe we can break the jinx this time."

They watched the screen intently as Kim Glass, one of Team USA's outside hitters, served the ball right into the net.

"Oh, no," Dina said. "I think the jinx is still on. Service errors are killin' us." She sighed and leaned back against the couch.

"If we're this nervous just watching a game on TV, how are we going to handle our first game on Tuesday?"

"Seriously." Dina took a handful of popcorn from her bowl to distract herself.

Brazil's serve rocketed over the net. Kim Glass set up under it perfectly and passed it to Team USA's setter, Lindsey Berg. Dina wasn't sure where Berg was going to put the set because Logan Tom was ready to attack from the left side, Danielle Scott-Arruda was ready in the middle, and Tayyiba Haneef-Park could pounce from the right side. Berg sent a short set up the middle. *Bam!* Scott-Arruda slammed the ball past the Brazil blockers to give Team USA the lead again by a 2-1 score.

"That was awesome," Dina said. "Sett—" She was about to say, "settuhs." "Setters don't get enough credit."

"Really, but I'm sure Brittany will make sure she gets more than her fair share of credit."

"Criminy, you're right."

Christine burst out laughing and held up her hand for a

high five. "Criminy. What the heck does that word mean, anyway?"

Dina shrugged. "Heck if I know. I'm new around here, 'member?"

After a few more well-played volleys, Team USA found themselves up by a score of 5-1 when a timeout was called.

"Hey, Dina?"

"Yeah?"

"Did you go to Temple today?"

"Yeah, this morning." Dina took a hefty swig from her water bottle. "Why?"

"Oh, I don't know," Christine said. "I was just—Well, I was wondering what it was like."

"Temple? Oh, I guess it's pretty much like when you go to church."

"Does your dad wear one of those beanie hats?"

Dina laughed. "You mean a yarmulke?"

Christine's eyes grew wide. "How do you pronounce it?"

"It's Yiddish. You pronounce it yah-mick-kuh."

"Yuhmickuh."

"Close enough," Dina said with a laugh. "My dad's in Kuwait now, but, yes, he wears one when we go to Temple. All the men and boys do. Covering your head shows respect for G-d."

"Can't you just wear a Chicago Cubs hat instead?"

"I think Rabbi Herzl would have a fit." Dina laughed again. "Baseball hats aren't exactly traditional."

"You don't celebrate Christmas, right?" Christine tried to sound nonchalant, but Dina could tell she thought not celebrating Christmas was the worst thing that could possibly happen to a person.

"No, we celebrate Chanukah. It's better because we get presents eight days in a row," Dina teased. "You guys just get one day."

"Fine." Christine narrowed her eyes playfully. "Rub that in."

"Back home on Long Island, we always said, 'Merry Kwanukahmas.'"

"Kwan-ooka-mas? What does that mean?"

"Kwanza, Chanukah, and Christmas all jumbled together. Kwanukahmas."

Christine laughed. "That's cool. I'll have to remember to say that in December."

"You should totally come over during Chanukah. My mom and I fry potato latkes, and we eat them with applesauce. You could even help us make them. I'm not sure what day Chanukah starts this year, but—"

"It's not on the same day every year like Christmas?"

Dina laughed again. "No, the Jewish calendar follows the cycles of the moon or somethin', so all the holidays like Rosh Hashanah, Yom Kippur, Sukkot, and Chanukah are on different days every year. They fall around the same time, though. Rosh Hashanah's coming up soon. In September."

"What's Rosh Hashanah?"

"The Jewish New Year." Dina laughed to herself because here they were supposedly watching the most important volleyball game in the world, and they were talking about Jewish holidays. She didn't mind. She was glad to share her faith with Christine. "I like Rosh Hashanah. We eat challah bread and dip it in honey."

"Why honey?"

"To hope for a good and sweet New Year."

"All your holidays are about food."

Dina laughed. "I guess so. Well, not Yom Kippur."

"Why not?"

"On Yom Kippur we fast for twenty-four hours."

Christine's eyes widened. "A whole day?"

"Seriously. A whole day. We can't eat or drink anything from sundown to sundown. I haven't fasted for Yom Kippur before, but now that I had my Bat Mitzvah, I have to do it. We're gonna eat a big family dinner right before Temple on the first night. That way we don't get so hungry."

"That sounds pretty harsh."

"Yom Kippur is supposed to be a day of atonement, anyway."

"What's that mean?"

"It's a day for prayer and reflection. We pray for G-d to forgive our sins against him and hope he won't judge us too harshly."

"You know what?" Christine nodded slightly.

"What?"

"Yom Kippur sounds like Lent. We have to give up stuff for forty days. I usually give up candy or soda or something."

"For forty days? Now *that's* harsh."

"Yeah, I guess you're right," Christine agreed.

A loud cheer came from the television, and they turned their attention back to the game.

"Look, look." Christine pointed at the TV. "We're winning 20-15."

"Do you think we can actually win this game?"

Christine shrugged. "Fingers crossed." She crossed her index and middle fingers on both hands.

"Fingers crossed." Dina crossed her fingers on both hands as well. "I hate that you already know who won."

Christine closed her lips tight in a wide grin.

Dina dropped a handful of popcorn in her lap, and Christine burst out laughing. "Get a grip, Dina."

Dina picked up each piece of popcorn one by one with her thumb and ring finger. "This is hard."

Once she got all the popcorn back in her bowl, she gave her full attention to the game. A Brazil player jump served the ball to Logan Tom in the back row. Tom passed it cleanly to Lauren Berg who popped up a picture-perfect set. Dina held her breath as Kim Glass smashed the ball onto the floor in Brazil territory.

"Whoo hoo," Dina yelled, pumping both hands in the air, fingers still crossed.

The USA team made a mistake and let Brazil get both the point and the serve back to make the score 21-16 with Team USA still in the lead. The ball sailed out of bounds, and the serve went right back to Team USA.

"See?" Christine pointed at the TV with her crossed fingers. "Even Brazil messes up their serves."

With the score now 22-16 in Team USA's favor, they were three points away from taking a set from the Brazil team, who hadn't lost one single set in the entire Olympic Games. Tayyiba Haneef-Park and Danielle Scott-Arruda skied high to put up a perfect block, scoring another Team USA point.

"Into the roof." Christine punched a fist into the air.

The next serve for Team USA went long, and Dina and Christine groaned. In true Team USA fashion, they got the point right back as Scott-Arruda's blast careened off the Brazil team's block and went out of bounds. Dina and Christine stood up with the score 24-17, ready to celebrate a sure Team USA win. One of the Brazil players leaped high over the lone USA blocker and smashed a sizzling kill for another point. With the score 24 -18, Brazil now had the serve.

Dina held her breath when both teams volleyed the next serve back and forth several times. A Brazil attacker leaped high and hit the ball hard over the net. Team USA's libero, Nicole Davis, dug the ball up and passed it to the front row. Lindsey Berg got under it.

"Set it to Logan," Dina called.

"To Logan," Christine shouted in agreement.

Berg popped the ball up in the air, and Logan Tom flew in from Jupiter to smash the ball over the net. It crashed to the floor for the winning point. Team USA won the second game in the best three out of five series.

Dina and Christine leaped high in the air and hugged each other. Dina forgot to keep her fingers crossed, but she didn't care. Team USA had just tied the match at one set apiece in the gold medal game.

"Phew," Christine said as she sat down. "I don't know if I can take much more of this. And I know what happens."

Dina blew out a sigh. "C'mon, let's make some more popcorn. We've got at least two more sets to go."

Chapter 12
West Morrill

Dina sat in a metal fold-up chair on the visitors' side of the court in the West Morrill gymnasium. Christine sat on one side while Brittany and Marguerite sat on the other. Dina searched the stands for her mom. Back home on Long Island, her mom went to every single game, but so far Dina hadn't spotted her. Hopefully, she hadn't gotten lost trying to find West Morrill Middle School. Her dad was still in Kuwait, and she wasn't sure when he was coming back.

She tapped Christine on the leg. "I can't believe how nervous I am."

"Me, too."

"Criminy," Brittany chimed in. "Once we start playing, I think we'll be okay."

"I hope so." Dina sighed.

"Oh." Brittany stood up. "My mom's here. C'mon, I want to introduce you."

"Me?" Dina asked.

"Yeah, c'mon." Brittany grabbed Dina's uniform sleeve and pulled.

Dina followed Brittany toward the stands. "Do we have time?"

"What? Yeah? Coach Matthews is still talking to the West Morrill coach."

"Okay." Dina let herself be led up the steps of the visitors' bleachers. Brittany's mother had the same platinum blonde hair as her daughter. Dina wondered if the color came from a bottle.

"Mom, this is Dina."

Dina smiled. "It's nice to meet—"

"Mom, she's Jewish," Brittany blurted as if presenting her mother with an exotic zoo animal.

Dina inhaled sharply, but Mrs. Nelson simply smiled with closed lips. "It's always nice to meet Brittany's friends. I love your gorgeous hair, so perfectly black. Is that natural?"

Dina nodded. Her hunch about the artificial blonde hair color was probably right.

Dina walked a few steps in front of Brittany as they hustled back to the team bench. She couldn't believe Brittany had just introduced her like that. How about just, "This is Dina," or "This is Dina, she's from New York"? She rolled her eyes.

Back on the team bench, Dina whispered to Christine how Brittany had introduced her. Christine shook her head. "Criminy, that girl needs to learn some manners."

Dina laughed. Christine always seemed to have a way of lightening the mood. Not for the first time, she was glad they were friends.

The PA announcer asked them to stand for the national anthem. Dina took a deep breath to help her refocus on the game. The team remained standing while the PA announcer called out the starting lineups. Thankfully, Brittany and Marguerite were called out before she was, so she knew what to do. The PA announcer leaned toward the microphone. "Starting at outside hitter for the Flyers, number fifteen, Adina Jacobs."

Dina ran over to the officials and lightly bumped fists with both of them and then bumped fists with the opposing team's coach. She ran to the end line to high-five her teammates. Because Christine was the libero, she was called last. Dina raised her hands as high as she could. Christine took the challenge and leaped. Their hands smacked together.

"Nice one, boss," Dina said with a smile.

Christine took her place at the end of the starting lineup.

Just as they were about to take the floor to start their game, Dina caught sight of her mother climbing into the stands. Her heart almost stopped when she saw her father, too. She'd know that tan overcoat and black hat anywhere. Everybody said she got her dark hair from him, but she also knew she got her big honkin' nose from him, too. Oh, well. Who cared? Her dad was home from Kuwait.

"Hi, Dad." She waved frantically. "Hi, Mom."

Her mother smiled and waved back. Her father took off his hat, placed it over his heart, and bowed to his daughter. "Good luck, *Chamudi*. Play well."

"Thanks, Dad."

Christine raised an eyebrow. "*Chamudi?*"

Dina felt herself blush. "That's his pet name for me. It means 'my cutie' in Hebrew."

"Okay, *Chamudi*." Christine laughed. "Have a great game."

"You, too," Dina called back over her shoulder and set up on the left side of the net.

Because Christine was the libero, she had to wait on the side of the court until the official checked the lineup and called her in. At the official's signal, Christine ran to the back row and waited for the serve from the West Morrill team. The ball floated over the net and fell in for an ace right behind Brittany. Point West Morrill. Dina wasn't sure why Brittany hadn't moved for the ball, but then remembered Christine complaining that Brittany thought setters only had to set.

"C'mon, Flyers," Christine called out. "We can do this."

The next serve from the West Morrill team went straight to Christine who passed it up to Brittany. Coach Matthews had called a play to set up Dina for the kill first thing. Dina took her approach, but Brittany's set was way off the net. Dina scrambled to salvage the play and hit the ball squarely into the net. Darn. Another point for West Morrill.

The game continued, and Dina felt bad for Christine because she dove left and right and forward and back in order to pass the ball up to Brittany. Brittany must have been more nervous than she let on. Her sets were all over the place, not like in practice when they were usually dead on. Dina wasn't the only one getting frustrated. Marguerite sighed more than usual. Dina's coach back home had told her once that some people were practice players, and others were game players. By the looks of it, Brittany was a practice player.

The Earhart Flyers finally got the side out for their serve and were losing by a whopping 1-6. Christine punched a floater serve that careened off a West Morrill player's upper arm in their back row, for the second Flyers point. The West Morrill team couldn't handle Christine's serves, and the Earhart Flyers scored two more points. With the score 4-6, the West Morrill team finally returned Christine's serve.

Christine got under the ball in the back row and passed it cleanly up to Brittany. Brittany back set the ball. The set was perfect, and Dina got that excited feeling in the pit of her stomach. She took her steps and leaped. She snapped her wrist and sent the ball smashing to the floor on the other side. All six West Morrill players stood in a circle and stared at the spot where Dina's kill had landed.

"Campfire," Brittany yelled toward the West Morrill team who looked more than a little stunned.

The Flyers formed a quick circle in the center of their side of the court. "Point," they yelled and leaned back. They put one hand on the floor and pointed the other at the ceiling.

Dina stood back up and looked at Christine. "What's a campfire?"

"That's when everybody stands in a circle looking at one spot on the floor. They look like they're staring at a campfire."

Dina laughed. "That is the craziest thing I've ever heard."

"Brittany said it. Not me."

"*Criminy*," Dina whispered, and Christine laughed. They ran back to their positions.

With the score 5-6 still in West Morrill's favor, Christine served the ball toward West Morrill's libero. Their libero passed the ball to her setter. West Morrill's opposite hitter began her approach to the net. Marguerite ran up next to Dina. They leaped hip-to-hip for the block. Dina's hands connected with the ball. It fell toward her and got tangled up in the net. She tried to pop it back up, but it got caught in the net again and fell to the ground. Another point for West Morrill.

Coach Matthews screeched for a time-out. The subs leaped up as if they didn't want to get caught in the crossfire. Dina scurried to the bench with her teammates. She snagged her water bottle and took a long swig.

Coach Matthews squatted down in front of them. "Good come back so far, girls. Maybe we've shaken out our first game jitters. Let's focus on our strengths now." She spun on the balls of her feet and faced Brittany. "Chase down those balls on their serve. You're our best setter, but we need your defense, too."

Brittany puffed up. Dina tried not to roll her eyes. Coach Matthews obviously knew how to stroke Brittany's ego enough to motivate her.

Coach Matthews looked at Dina and then Marguerite. "Dina. Marguerite. Next time you jump up for the block, get closer to the net and keep your hands turned toward the center of the court, so the ball deflects onto their court and not out of bounds. And if the ball falls on our side again, wait for it to drop down off the net and then pop it back up. Easier said than done, I know."

Dina and Marguerite nodded.

The Flyers ran back onto the court after the time-out. Dina waved to her parents. She had mixed feelings. She wanted the game over fast, so she could run over to hug her dad, but she loved playing volleyball so much she never wanted it to end.

The West Morrill team made several runs, and although the Flyers made admirable comebacks each time, they were always too little and too late. The Earhart Flyers lost the first set 14-25 and then went on to lose the second set 18-25. Dina wished they played three out of five like the Olympic team instead of just two out of three, because she felt like her team was just getting warmed up.

Dina sat on the bench next to Christine and pulled off her court sneakers. "I dunno why we played so bad." She jammed her sneakers and pads into her equipment bag. "We couldn't catch any breaks."

Christine nodded her agreement. "Just like Team USA. They had to be happy with silver when they didn't catch any breaks against Brazil in the gold medal game."

Dina smacked Christine lightly on the arm. "I can't believe you knew Team USA got the silver all along and didn't tell me."

Christine smiled at her cross-eyed.

Dina returned the cross-eyed look, and they both laughed.

"They've never won the gold," Christine said. "At least Logan Tom won the Best Scorer award, right?"

"Yeah, that's cool."

"And in 2020, when Dina Jacobs and Christine Hannigan make the Olympic team, it'll be gold for sure."

"Seriously," Dina said. "Someday." She zipped her equipment bag shut and leaped up. "C'mon, let me introduce you to my dad."

"Okay, just don't introduce me as your Catholic friend."

"Deal." Dina stuck out her hand, and Christine shook it vigorously.

Chapter 13
G-d in the Backseat

Dina dropped her volleyball bag on the gym floor and gave her mother and father hugs.

"When'd you get back, Dad?" She kept one arm wrapped around him.

"Your mother picked me up from the Indianapolis Airport around two o'clock." He smiled at her and then turned to smile at Christine.

"Oh, sorry, Dad. This is my friend, Christine."

"Very nice to meet you, young lady." He put his hand out, and they shook hands. A quizzical look crossed his face. "Young lady, what do you have behind your ear?"

"What?" Christine ran both hands over both ears. "What is it?" She looked at Dina for help.

Dina bit down hard to keep from laughing.

"Here, let me see if I can get it." Her father slipped his right hand behind Christine's left ear. "Ah, here we go." He held out a silver coin about the size of a quarter between his thumb and index finger.

Christine's mouth fell open. "How did you . . . ?"

Dina burst out laughing. "Now he has somebody else to do that trick on."

Her father handed the coin to Christine.

"Oh, I can't take that, Mr. Jacobs."

"Sure you can. That's a fifty-fils Kuwait coin. It's not worth much, and we have plenty. In fact, I have a dozen more waiting in the car for my *Chamudi*." He smiled at Dina. "I knew you'd be impatient to see them, so I brought a couple in." He took another coin from his pocket and handed it to her.

Dina gave her father another quick hug. "Thanks, Dad."

"We'd better get Daddy home." Her mother herded the group toward the exit. "He's still on Kuwait time."

Her father sighed. "That's true. It's three o'clock in the morning for me right now." He plunked his old-fashioned black hat on his head.

"Wait, Mom," Dina said. "I have to tell Coach Matthews that I'm not going back on the bus, and I have to get my backpack, too."

"Okay, go on."

Dina ran to Coach Matthews where she was talking to one of the officials. She waited patiently off to one side.

"Okay, Margo," Coach Matthews said to the official. "I'll see you at the next one."

"You got it." The official threw on her jacket and headed toward the exit.

Coach Matthews turned around. "Oh, Dina. I didn't see you there. What's up?"

"I'm going home with my folks, okay?" Dina gestured to where they were standing by the door with Christine.

"Oh. Is it okay if I meet my star player's family?"

Dina felt her face get warm at the compliment. "Okay." She led the way across the gym. "Mom, Dad? This is Coach Matthews."

"It's nice to meet you, Mr. and Mrs. Jacobs." Coach Matthews put her hand out.

"Doctor," Dina said.

Coach Matthews finished shaking Dina's father's hand and took Dina's mother's outstretched hand. "Doctor?" She looked perplexed for a moment, until something seemed to dawn on her. "Oh, I'm sorry. Dr. and Mrs. Jacobs."

"No, it's—" Dina started.

"Actually," her mother interrupted, "I'm Dr. Jacobs, Assistant Professor of Environmental Science at Purdue. So it's Mr. and Dr. Jacobs."

"Oh," Coach Matthews said, "sorry about that."

Dina was surprised to see Coach Matthews's cheeks turning red from embarrassment.

"It's all right," her father said with a wink. "It happens all the time."

Coach Matthews nodded. "So, uh, Dina will be going home with you, then?"

"Yes, if that's okay," Dina's mother said.

"Oh, absolutely, but I can't let Christine go with you this time. One of her parents would have to write a note giving you permission."

"Oh, that's okay, Coach," Christine said. "My mom's picking me up at school anyway." She looked at Dina. "Maybe tomorrow, though."

"Yeah." Dina nodded.

They headed out to the parking lot together.

"Dina is quite an athlete," Coach Matthews said.

"Thank you," Dina's mother said. "She enjoys volleyball."

"Well, good. I see a bright future for her in the sport." Coach Matthews veered off toward the bus. "I guess I'll see you all again tomorrow at Turpin Prairie Middle School."

"We'll be there," Dina's mother said.

"Okay. Take care." Coach Matthews headed toward the bus.

"Christine," Dina's mother said, "I'll call your mom when I get home, but ask her to write a note giving us permission to take you home from Turpin Prairie tomorrow."

"Okay, I will. Thanks. She usually comes to my home games, but she says my brother's too much of a handful at away games." She turned rather shyly to Dina's father. "Thanks for the Kuwait coin."

"You're welcome, young lady. I'm glad my *Chamudi* has made such a nice new friend here."

Dina smiled at Christine's blush.

"See you tomorrow, Dina." Christine headed toward the yellow school bus.

Dina ran after her. "Wait, I have to get my backpack off the bus."

They walked to the bus together, and Christine hopped up on the first step. "Wait here. I'll go get it."

"Okay."

Christine produced the backpack in record time.

"Thanks."

"No problem, *Chamudi*."

Dina stuck her tongue out at Christine and headed toward her waiting parents. "Big game tomorrow," Dina called back. "Turpin Prairie won't know what hit 'em."

Christine laughed and waved one last time before hopping back onto the bus.

Dina threw her volleyball bag and backpack into the backseat and got in. Her mother pulled the Crown Victoria out of the parking spot and headed toward the school's exit. Her father turned around in the passenger seat and handed her a brown paper bag.

The bag was heavy. "Coins?" Dina asked.

He nodded. "Only the finest for my soon-to-be world famous anthropologist daughter."

"Thanks, Dad." She opened the bag carefully and found a jumble of Kuwait coins. She pulled a few out and admired them. "How come so many?"

"Oh, I took the change out of my pockets everyday and threw them into this bag for you. There's a coffee shop near the hotel, and Baahir picked out the best quality coins for you every morning."

"He did?" Her father always told her about the cool people he met on his trips. His stories were the main reason she wanted to be a world traveler like him. "Tell him thanks next time you see him."

"I will."

Dina stuffed the bag of new coins into her backpack in the same pouch that still held the velvet bags of coins from her Show-and-Tell the Friday before. When she found a second, she'd sort through them and put them in her safe. Maybe she'd do it after Temple on Saturday.

"Someday, *Chamudi*, you can meet Baahir yourself. We'll get coffee at his shop, and then I'll take you and your mother to the Scientific Center in Salmiya."

Dina knew her dad would make good on his promise. He had brought home a brochure from the Scientific Center once when they still lived on Long Island, and Robyn had grabbed it out of her hands before she'd even had a chance to look at it. Robyn wanted to be a marine biologist, and thought the aquarium looked cool. She wondered why Robyn always made fun of her dream to travel all over the world, when she'd never once made fun of Robyn's dream.

As soon as they got home, Dina decided to run over to Robyn's house to show her the new Kuwait coins. Pain squeezed her heart when she remembered. Robyn didn't live two blocks away anymore. Robyn lived over eight hundred miles away now.

Dina sat silently in the dark backseat, remembering the old Jewish saying that G-d was closest to those with broken hearts. If that was the case, then G-d was right there in the backseat with her, because her heart was breaking all over again.

Chapter 14
Star City

Dina pulled up her knee pads, glad they finally had a game in their own gym. So far the Earhart Middle School seventh grade volleyball team hadn't won a single game. She waited for the PA announcer to call her name. When he did, she ran onto the court, punched fists with the officials and the coach of the other team, and high-fived her teammates on the end line. She held her hands high when Christine ran onto the court. Christine's leaped and hit Dina's hands with a resounding smack.

"You're getting good at that."

"I'm pretending I'm Blair Bashen, and I play for Purdue."

"Cool. I'm Kristen Arthurs then, 'cept she plays middle, and I play outside." Dina slid over to her spot on the floor. "Maybe I'm Carrie Gurnell."

"You could be both wrapped up in one."

"Seriously."

Dina jumped up and down a few times to get her nerves under control. The ultra-tall girls on the Star City team made her ultra-nervous. On top of that, Christine told her that Star City was their biggest rival, so Dina was prepared to hate them. She felt a little bad, though, because she didn't know any of the Star City players, but she knew all about rivalries because her dad was an avid Yankees fan.

"You can't like both the Yankees and the Red Sox," her dad always said. "You have to choose one or the other." So, naturally, Dina chose to cheer for the Yankees. And, besides, Derek Jeter and ARod were kind of cute, so it was easy to hate the Red Sox. But here in West Lafayette, Indiana she didn't quite understand the rivalry yet.

"C'mon, Flyers," Christine called from the back row.

A Star City player served the ball over the net to start the first game. Christine passed the ball cleanly to Brittany, but Brittany set the ball too close to the net. Dina scrambled and dinked it over. The blockers knocked it right back. Point Star City.

"They read your body language," Coach Matthews hissed at Dina. "Don't give yourself away. Fool the defense by hitting at them hard, hard, hard. Then tap one over. C'mon now. Use your head."

Dina knew she couldn't answer back, but Coach Matthews must've seen Brittany's bad set. She took a deep breath and tried to focus. Coach Matthews must be cranky because in a little over a week they had lost their first three games.

Everything seemed to go wrong for the Flyers in that first set. Even though Christine scored a few points with her moving floater serve, the rest of the team couldn't get its act together. Brittany especially had trouble getting her sets in the right place. Dina knew something was seriously wrong when Marguerite stamped her foot in frustration at one of Brittany's lousy sets.

Dina slammed herself into a chair after losing the first set by a miserable score of 4-25. She was so embarrassed that she didn't even wave at her mom and dad in the stands. She was surprised when Marguerite sat down next to her.

"I'm so embarrassed," Marguerite whispered.

"Me, too." Dina took a long drink from her water bottle and then wiped the sweat off her face with her towel.

Marguerite leaned closer and said in a low voice, "Brittany's sucking wind today. I mean, c'mon, how are we supposed to get any decent hits?" She stifled a laugh. Dina hid her face in the towel to hide her laughter.

"Girls," Coach Matthew snapped. "I'm so glad you think this is funny."

Startled, Dina straightened up. She registered the glare on Coach Matthews face loud and clear. Marguerite must have seen it, too, because she stopped smiling and lowered her head.

Coach Matthews paced in front of them. "Look, girls. I've said this before. This is our home court. There is no way we should be losing this badly to this team. They're a good team," she poked the air toward the Star City team, "but so are we." She looked at Dina and Marguerite and the other hitters on the team. "You big girls have got to find a way to get some power into your hits. We only had one kill in the first set, for goodness sakes. One. And we got the other three points because the other team made mistakes. Something has to change, ladies."

Dina looked at Brittany out of the corner of her eye. If only Brittany could get them some decent sets.

"Look, girls, there's no such thing as a bad set," Coach Matthews said, as if reading Dina's thoughts. "You simply have to make something out of it. Don't start playing the blame game."

The official blew the whistle to start the second set.

Coach Matthews shrugged. "Okay, girls. It's up to you now."

Dina blew out a sigh and found her position on the court. Hopefully this game would start off better.

It didn't. Brittany set up all her teammates except Dina and Marguerite. With the score 0-5 in Star City's favor, Coach Matthews screeched for a time-out.

Once the team sat on the bench, Coach Matthews pointed at Brittany. "I don't know what's going on between you three," she moved her finger to include Dina and Marguerite, "but it ends here. Now. Brittany, you are the best setter I've seen on a seventh grade team in a long, long time. In fact, you're probably good enough to play on the eighth grade team, but you wouldn't know it today." She looked at the floor for a second and took a deep breath. "Look, you guys are not playing up to your potential." She moved her gaze from player to player, substitutes included. "I don't know who you people are, but I want my team back. I want the athletes back that I trained for this day." She smacked her hands together. "Go find them." She pointed at the court and turned away.

Dina slinked back onto the court with her teammates.

Christine called all the players together. "C'mon, you guys.

We can do this." The players put their hands together in the team circle. "Flyers on three. One, two, three."

"Flyers," the team yelled.

Marguerite high-fived Brittany. "C'mon Britt. We can do this, okay? Let's kick some Star City butt."

Brittany didn't make eye contact with Marguerite for a few tense moments, but then she finally gave in. "Whatev."

Brittany finally found her groove and put up some tasty sets for both Dina and Marguerite. They even tried a quick short set play they had been working on in practice. Dina loved those. The Star City team seemed surprised every single time, like they'd never seen a short set. Dina lost track, but figured she and Marguerite made about fifteen kills between them in the second set.

The score was 24-22 in the Flyers favor when Dina's turn came back up to serve. She wanted to serve an ace to win the set and force a third. She got her feet set, tossed the ball up, brought her arm though and snapped her wrist. As soon as she made contact, she knew the hit was bad. The ball floated weakly into the net. Point Star City. Side out Star City.

"That's okay," Christine called to her. "You'll get 'em next time."

Dina wasn't so sure.

The Star City player stepped behind the end line and got ready to serve.

"Dina, I'm setting you up," Brittany whispered. "Smash it from the back row, okay?"

"Okay." Dina's stomach tumbled. They hadn't had much practice with hits from behind the ten-foot line. She knew she had to leap high like Logan Tom and Kristen Arthurs if she was going to do it right.

The Star City serve came over the net, and, as promised, Brittany set the ball up to Dina in the back row. She felt that familiar tingle in her stomach and leaped high in the air. She brought her arm down, and she snapped her wrist. The contact felt perfect, but for one time-stopping moment she watched the ball hit the tape on the top of the net and threaten to stay on their side. Luck was with her, though, and the ball trickled over the top and landed onto Star City's floor.

The official blew her whistle. The Flyers had just won the second set.

Christine ran over and hugged Dina.

Dina hugged her back. "That was so close."

Christine didn't have a chance to respond because Brittany and Marguerite and the rest of the team swarmed Dina. They patted her on the back and high-fived her. With huge smiles, Dina and Christine walked arm-in-arm to the end line. Once the official released them, they sprinted to the team bench.

Coach Matthews wore a rare smile. "Now *that's* the team I've coached this year." She nodded, obviously pleased with her players. "But we can't rest on our laurels. We have one more set to go, so keep up that energy. Make sure you drink some water." She walked to the end of the bench to talk with Dr. Lewiski, the school's athletic director.

Dina got a troubled feeling in her stomach when she noticed Coach Matthews and the athletic director looking directly at her.

Chapter 15
Operation Shakedown

In an exciting third and final set, the Flyers beat Star City by a tiebreaker score of 15-13. Dina and Christine linked arms and skipped their way into the locker room.

They chanted, "Go Flyers. It's your birthday. Star City. It's your lose-day," over and over again.

Christine continued to sing as Dina stopped and opened her locker. She pulled out her backpack and set it on the bench. Christine linked arms with Dina again, and they swung around the locker room. Trying to avoid crashing into Marguerite, Dina bumped into her backpack and knocked it over. Her books and supplies scattered across the locker room floor.

"Oh, crap." She put both hands on her head. "Why did I leave it unzipped?"

"Who cares?" Christine said. "We just beat Star City."

Dina picked up her math book and jammed it into the nearly empty backpack.

Christine bent down and picked up the brown velvet bags containing Dina's foreign coins. "I can't believe those five-hundred-yen coins are worth five dollars each. They look like plain old quarters. Can I look at one?"

"Sure, open the drawstring and dump them out."

Christine sat down and eased all the coins onto the bench. She sorted through the overflowing mound while Dina picked up the contents of her backpack from the floor. "Hey, where are the five-hundred yens? You had two of them, right?"

"Yeah." Dina stopped stuffing books into her backpack to look through the coins on the bench. "Oh, c'mon. No way."

She re-checked the coins. Nothing. She put her hand in each velvet bag. All of them were empty.

"They're not here." She unzipped her backpack and dumped

out all the books and notebooks she had just stuffed in. No coins. The floor and surrounding area also revealed nothing.

"Huh," Dina said. "That's really weird. Let me see if any of my other coins are missing."

Christine helped Dina carefully separate the coins on the bench. "I'm missing three coins total."

"Are you sure?"

"Yeah, both five-hundred-yen coins and the new ten shekalim from Israel."

"Are you sure?"

"Yeah, the new ten shekalim had the palm tree on it. I liked that one. It's worth about two dollars and fifty cents."

"Do you think somebody took them?" Christine sounded like she had her suspicions.

Dina shrugged. She felt the sting of tears starting and wiped them away.

"Oh, don't cry." Christine put her arm around her as they sat side-by-side on the bench. "We'll figure something out. Okay?"

Dina took a deep breath. "Okay." She was so glad she and Christine were friends. She had been riding high after the big win over Star City, but now her hands were shaking. She loved those coins. "I'm so stupid. I should have checked after my Show-and-Tell to make sure I got 'em all back." And she should have put every single one of them back in her safe that same day. She mentally kicked herself.

Christine sat at her desk in Mr. Robertson's classroom, clutching the framed photograph of her Aunt Christine. She spun around in her seat. "Did you find your coins?"

Dina pressed her lips together tightly and shook her head. "Nope."

"Operation Shakedown then?"

Dina nodded. "Operation Shakedown."

They bumped fists, and Christine turned back around.

Mr. Robertson stood up from behind his desk. "Christine, are you ready?"

Christine nodded. "Yup." She leaped to her feet.

She got to the front of the room and held out the framed photograph of her aunt. "This is my Aunt Christine. I'm named after her. You can tell by her uniform that she's in the army. Well, she's in the reserves, and she's currently stationed in Kuwait."

"Christine," Mr. Robertson said, "this is a very fitting Show-and-Tell for Patriot's Day."

"Thanks." Christine turned back to the class. "I'm going to tell you all about my aunt and the war in a sec, but first, Dina wanted me to tell you that three of her coins are missing. They probably just fell out of her backpack or something, but she wanted me to tell you that they're pretty worthless, and you can't use them in a store or anything. In fact, they're only good if you exchange them at a Currency Converter Bank, but that won't do you any good either because Dina's dad reported the serial numbers to the authorities already."

Dina recited the multiplication tables in her head, so she wouldn't burst out laughing. Coins didn't have serial numbers. She chanced a look at Mr. Robertson. He had an amused smile on his face, but he didn't say anything. She was surprised when he turned his head slightly and winked at her. He must have figured out what they were trying to do.

"So if you tried to convert the coins to U.S. money," Christine continued, "you'd get arrested in a heartbeat and sent straight to Japan or Israel or Syria for your trial. My Aunt Christine told me that in some Middle Eastern countries, they chop off your hand if you get caught stealing." She pulled her right hand into the sleeve of her sweatshirt and held up the handless sleeve for emphasis. "And believe me, my aunt would know because she's there right now."

Dina snuck a peak at Aaron and Tyler. Christine said she was sure one of them had taken the coins. Tyler looked as cool as a cucumber, but Aaron sat stone still. Dina wasn't sure how to read him.

"So if anyone happens to find the coins lying around, please give them to Dina," Mr. Robertson added, "or drop them off on my desk. Okay?"

Dina kept her eyes on Aaron. He nodded slightly, and she wondered if Christine had been right when she said Aaron was their leading suspect. She wasn't so sure, because a lot of the other students nodded, too.

"Okay, Christine, carry on," Mr. Robertson said.

Christine turned her attention back to the class and told them about her aunt's experiences as a reservist in the U.S. army. She even wrote her aunt's Kuwait address on the whiteboard in case anyone wanted to write to her.

Christine finished her presentation and sat down.

Dina leaned forward. "You were great. I think I'll write to your aunt tonight."

"I can't wait for you to meet her." Christine leaned in and said in a low voice, "So do you think Operation Shakedown is going to work?"

"Seriously? Yeah. It's just a matter of time."

Dina punched fists with Christine. She couldn't wait to see how fast the coins appeared on Mr. Robertson's desk.

Chapter 16

Detrash the Wabash

Two weeks after Operation Shakedown had begun, Dina's missing coins still had not appeared on Mr. Robertson's desk or anywhere else for that matter. She pulled at her rubber gloves and sighed. She had so many things to think about. Her coins, for one, but bigger than that, she had to tell Coach Matthews she couldn't play in the game against St. Agnes Catholic on Friday because of Rosh Hashanah.

She was not looking forward to that moment, especially since the team was on a two-game winning streak. Coach Matthews had gotten more intense than usual during practice, and Dina was sure she would explode when she heard about Rosh Hashanah.

With a poke of her trash stabber, Dina impaled a burger wrapper and thrust it into the plastic bag hanging off her belt loop. She took a deep breath and inhaled the cool autumn air. Focusing on the debris on the banks of the Wabash River was much more fun than focusing on her troubles.

She looked up and saw Christine trying to dig something out of the mud. "Hey, Christine. What did you find?"

Christine looked up. "I don't know. It's rusty metal of some sort."

Dina abandoned her section of shoreline and scurried over. "I'm so glad we didn't have practice today, so we could do this with my mom and her students."

"Uh, yeah, sure." Christine rolled her eyes. "I just love to detrash the Wabash every September. Ah, it brings back memories of when I was a child—"

"Oh, shuddup." Dina backhanded Christine playfully on the arm. "You didn't havta come, yuh know." She bugged out her eyes.

"I'm just kidding."

"I know. Sorry. I'm kind of cranky today, I guess." Dina kicked at the rusty object embedded in the ground. "Do you think it's a car?"

"That'll take a year to dig out."

"Seriously." Dina used her trash stabber to poke around the object.

"Do they really clean up the river every year?" Christine used her own trash stabber to move the mud away from the metal. "Hey, this looks like a box of some kind."

So far all Dina could see was a rusty corner. "I think so. My mom said they have this Green Week on the Purdue campus in April—"

"Green? Like environmental green?"

"Yeah, but my mom said caring for the environment should be more than a once a year thing." Dina pushed a big clump of mud away. "Look at the faded red paint on it."

"Not much left."

"We should have a Green Week at Earhart Middle."

"Maybe we can do it in April. You know, the same week Purdue has theirs?" Christine started to kneel down in the mud, but made a face and quickly stood back up. "What should we do?"

"For Green Week?"

Christine nodded.

"We could put up posters that say, 'Think Green.'"

"Or, 'Love your mother.'"

"Love your muthuh?"

Christine laughed. "You lost another r."

"Oops, sorry." Dina smiled. "I'm working on it. I promise. So, what was that about loving your mother?"

"Mother Earth."

"Oh." Dina laughed. "We'd have to draw a picture of the Earth, though, 'cuz nobody's going to get that."

"Yeah, you're probably right."

"My mom says last year the Purdue students were challenged to take three-minute showers during Green Week."

"Three minutes? There's no way I can take, like, a three-minute shower." Christine looked at Dina as if she had three heads.

"Yes, you can. My mom challenged me, and the first time it took me three whole minutes to get the water the right temperature, but I figured out a better strategy for the next time."

"What? Stay dirty?"

"Ha ha. Hey, poke your stabber thingy on the other side, and I'll work mine on this side. I can't wait to see what this is." Dina dug in with her stabber. "So, anyway, I figured out that you can wash stuff like your arms and feet while the water's getting warm. Once it's warm then you can wash the rest of you. The second time I made the mistake of using the same amount of shampoo that I always use. It took me, seriously, like, twelve minutes to rinse it all out."

"My mom always says, 'Use a quarter-sized amount, blah, blah, blah.'" Christine mimicked her mother. "I always forget."

"My mom told me the same thing, but, you know what?"

"What?"

"That's all you really need."

"I know." Christine scraped away at the mud encapsulating the rusty object and pushed her stabber underneath. "Hey, I'm under. Let me push up on it." She used her pole like a lever and pushed down hard. The rusty object loosened a bit, but stayed stuck.

"Here, let me get my pole underneath, too." Dina moved around Christine. With their combined strength, they managed to loosen the object enough to pop it out of the ground.

Christine threw her stabber to one side and gripped the rusty red box about the size of a shoe box. She grimaced as she swiped the mud off with her gloved hands. She held it away from her at arms' length. "What is this?"

"I have no idea. Hey, Mom?" Dina called. Her mother

was near the shoreline, picking up trash with a group of her Purdue environmental science students. "Look what we found."

"I'll be right over," her mother called. She stood taller than most of the students surrounding her except for a dark-haired guy wearing a Purdue weightlifting t-shirt. Dina tried not to laugh as her mother's students followed behind her like little ducklings.

Her mother and the students circled around them.

"What did you find, Christine?" Dina's mother said.

"I don't know." Christine turned the metal box around. "What do you think it is?"

Dina's mother took the box from Christine. "This looks like an old-fashioned cookie tin."

Dina made a sour face. "Do you think there are any cookies still in it?"

"Ewww." Christine shuddered.

Dina's mother handed the box back to Christine. "Why don't you girls open it?"

"You found it, Christine," Dina said. "How about I hold it, and you lift the top off."

"Okay."

The students crowded closer.

Christine carefully tugged at one side of the tin. It wouldn't budge. "I can't . . ." She thought about it for a second. "Wait, let me try wiggling both sides." She worked at one side and then the other. Finally, after several failed attempts, the top moved, and she wrestled it off. A stack of wet, mushy cardboard flyers sat in a layer of mud.

"Dr. Jacobs, what are these things?" Christine pulled out the wad of paper.

"I'm really not sure."

"Dr. Jacobs?" a blonde girl interrupted. "These look like flyers from the Knickerbocker Saloon for either an Indy 500 or a Brickyard 400 party. I can see the race car, but I can't read the rest."

Dina wasn't sure what a brickyard party was, but she didn't care. She'd heard the word saloon. "A saloon?" She pictured an old western town with gunslingers, whiskey on the bar, and tumbleweeds rolling through the streets past horses and stagecoaches.

"The Knickerbocker is supposedly Indiana's oldest bar," the blonde student continued, "and it's still open on Fifth Street. It's not just a bar anymore, either. They serve lunch and dinner, too. They have the best Nachos Cubanos in the world." The other students agreed.

"Really? Can we go, Mom? We can bring them the flyers and see if they want them back."

"Well, I doubt they want them back, but, sure, we can go there for dinner. Let's go home and pick up your dad." She pointed to Christine's muddy hands and forearms. "We need to get you girls cleaned up, too."

Christine nodded in agreement.

Dina's mother turned to her students. "I think we've detrashed enough of the Wabash for today."

The students looked relieved that their workday was just about over as they went about gathering up the equipment and putting the full trash bags in a designated spot in the parking lot. "Thank you, my faithful students. I'll see you all in class on Monday."

They said their respective goodbyes, and Dina's mother herded Dina and Christine toward her car. She opened the trunk and took out a few old towels, so they could get as much mud off their clothes as possible before actually getting in the car. "Christine, call your parents to make sure it's okay that you go to the Knickerbocker with us."

"You can shower at my house," Dina said, gesturing at Christine's still muddy clothes.

Christine held her arms out and looked herself over. "Yeah, I'm kind of yucky. Can I borrow some clothes?"

"They might be too big for you."

"That's okay."

"We're only allowed three minute showers at my house," Dina said, holding back a smile.

"You can time me."

"Oh, I will. Believe me." They bumped fists.

Dina and Christine showered up in record time at Dina's house, and now sat across from Dina's parents at the Knickerbocker Saloon waiting for the flat bread pizzas they had ordered. A lot of the food items on the Knickerbocker menu contained pork, including the Nachos Cubanos that the students had recommended, but since Dina's family tried to eat kosher whenever possible, they steered clear.

A mirrored bar with a bunch of colorful liquor bottles took up one whole wall of the saloon. Dark wood and ornate crown molding surrounded the mirrors and reminded Dina of a genuine old-timey saloon, except for all the regular people eating dinner there.

Christine nudged Dina's side. "Here comes the manager."

A man who looked to be in his late twenties with a crisp white shirt and black chinos walked up to their table. His thin mustache made Dina think he was trying to look older than he really was. He smiled at her parents, but addressed Dina and Christine. "So your server Mary says you found something of ours on the banks of the Wabash?"

Christine nodded and lifted up the plastic shopping bag containing the old cookie tin. "We found it today when we were cleaning up." She handed the manager the bag.

He pulled a chair over to their table and sat down. He lifted the cookie tin out of the bag and nudged off the top. He sat back with a smile. "Well, I'll be . . ."

"What are they?" Dina asked.

He smiled. "My nephew was supposed to hand out this stack of flyers in town last spring for the Indy 500 party we were hosting here. I remember putting them in this old tin."

"So what happened?" Dina asked.

The manager shrugged. "I guess he tossed them in the river."

"And then you girls found it four months later," Dina's dad added.

The manager nodded. "Apparently he got lazy and didn't want to hand them out." He pursed his lips together. "I can't wait to show my sister this. His mother."

"So what exactly is the Indy 500?" Dina asked.

Christine's jaw fell open. "You really are an alien. I knew it."

The manager laughed and said, "You folks must be new in town." He looked at Christine. "I'll leave you to explain it to her." He stood up and put the chair back. "Thanks so much for retrieving the tin. Oh, and your dinner? It's on me."

"Oh, you don't have to—" Dina's father started to say.

"No worries, folks. Enjoy your meal." He headed back toward the kitchen, the bag dangling loosely from his hand.

"Nice young man," Dina's mother said.

Dina's father nodded in agreement. A lock of his jet black hair fell into his eye, and he brushed it away with a practiced hand. "So, *Chamudi*, should we invite Christine over for Rosh Hashanah dinner?"

Christine looked at Dina hopefully. "Can I?"

"You want to eat Challah and dip apples in honey?"

Christine nodded. "Yeah. It'd be, like, really cool to see what a Jewish New Year is all about."

Dina's father tapped the table. "It's all settled then. One more for dinner, Dr. Jacobs." He smiled at Dina's mother.

"Okay, it's done."

Dina never had a friend over for Rosh Hashanah before. Back home, Robyn was always home with her own family. She was about to get really excited about Christine coming over, when she remembered.

"Actually," she said sheepishly, "she can't."

"Why not?" The disappointment in Christine's voice was obvious.

"We have a game against St. Agnes Christian that night. You

have to go, but I have to tell Serg—I mean, Coach Matthews that I can't go to the game."

"Do you want me to call your coach?" her mother said.

For a quick second Dina thought about taking her mother up on her offer. "No, Mom, it's my responsibility."

"That's my girl." Her father raised his water glass in a toast. "To taking responsibility."

Dina, Christine, and Dina's mother clinked glasses.

"So," her father continued, "speaking of taking responsibility. How are the three minute showers coming?"

"My record is two minutes and fifty seconds." Dina sat up taller.

"I came in at four minutes and twenty seconds today at your house," Christine said with a frown.

"That's really good for your first try. It gets easier as you go. I promise," Dina said with a smile.

She did have a lot to smile about, even though her afternoon had been filled with heavy thoughts about missing coins and drill sergeant volleyball coaches. Sitting at a table with her family and a friend in Indiana's oldest saloon made her problems fade away for a while.

Chapter 17

Supernova

Dina squatted low and placed her hands in front of her. She nodded at Christine to let her know she was ready. Christine tossed the ball up to herself and then smashed it toward the ground in front of Dina. Dina lunged, snagged a piece of the ball, and rolled using the new shoulder roll technique Coach Matthews had taught them.

"Dina!" Coach Matthews barked. "Get lower for those digs. C'mon, bend those knees. Dig and roll. Let's do another one." She grabbed a ball from the bin and practically shoved Christine out of the way. She smashed the ball down toward Dina.

Dina reached out with one arm, but it glanced weakly off her wrist. She finished her roll and looked up to find the ball bouncing feebly away.

"Again!" Coach Matthews barked.

Dina wanted to groan out loud, but didn't dare. This would be her tenth dig and roll in a row. Nobody else had done that many, but she didn't have time to complain. She squatted low. Coach Matthews smashed the ball. Dina took a quick step to her right, reached down with a strong right hand and popped the ball up. As she finished her roll, she was glad to see that Brittany had been able to set the ball cleanly. Despite that one good thing, she couldn't help the sting of tears in her eyes. Both she and Christine naively thought their practices would be a little more laid back after they had beaten Digby in two straight sets the day before, but Coach Matthews hadn't cracked a smile in two hours.

"Dina, you have a lot more work to do on those." Coach Matthews turned away and instructed the manager to put the balls away. She turned back to Dina who was still sitting on the floor with her head hung low. "You're better than that."

Christine, Marguerite, and Brittany flocked around Dina as if to protect her from further abuse. Dina, fighting back tears, refused to let on that Coach Matthews had worn her down. Christine seemed to know, though, and put her arm around her.

"Circle up, girls," Coach Matthews snapped.

Dina leaped to her feet, and the team formed a circle around their coach.

"Girls," Coach Matthews said, "beating Digby yesterday let me know that you have what it takes to win. It's still early yet, but if we keep this up we're almost guaranteed a spot in the Lafayette League Tournament at the end of the season. I'm especially proud of the way you beat Star City last Wednesday to start off our winning streak." She leaned in close and said in a low voice as if she didn't want anyone else in the gym to hear. "Even the eighth grade team couldn't beat Star City. They lost in two pitiful sets." She pulled back and continued in a normal voice. "Okay, tomorrow we annihilate Monon Middle School here at home and then Friday evening we bring St. Agnes Catholic down to their knees."

Dina sucked in a breath. Friday evening at sundown was the start of Rosh Hashanah. Her family would be in Temple. Somehow she had to find a way to tell Coach Matthews she couldn't make the Friday game. She almost wished she had taken her mother up on the offer to call the coach. Why she wanted to face the drill sergeant on her own was lost to her now. Maybe she could fake being sick on Friday and not go to school. They weren't allowed to play in a game if they didn't go to school.

"Hands in." Coach Matthews put her hand in the center of the circle. The girls piled their hands on top. "Flyers on three. One, two, three."

"Flyers," the girls yelled.

"See you all tomorrow." Coach Matthews dismissed the team.

Dina, Christine, Marguerite, and Brittany headed toward the locker room. Dina wanted to cling to the get-sick-on-Friday scheme, but knew she couldn't. She had to talk to Coach Matthews. Now.

Christine put an arm around Dina's shoulder. "She picked on you big time today."

"Seriously," Dina said. "What the heck did I do?"

"Criminy," Brittany added, "she must be on her period or something."

Marguerite stifled a giggle.

"Brittany," Christine grimaced, "that's disgusting."

"Hey, it could be true."

Dina tried to laugh with her friends, but she couldn't. She stopped walking. "Hey, guys, I'll catch up with you in a minute. I have to, uh . . ." A wave of nerves shot through her and closed her throat.

"What's wrong?" Christine asked. "Are you okay?"

"Yeah. I just . . ." Her mouth went dry. "I just havta tell Coach Matthews about Rosh Hashanah, and she's not gonna like it."

Christine's eyes grew wide. "Omigosh. That's right. You have to go to Temple on Friday when we play St. Agnes Catholic. Yikes."

"Criminy. She's going to lay you out flat when you tell her. Want us to wait?" Brittany looked as scared as Dina felt.

"No." Her three friends started to walk toward the locker room, but the thought of facing Coach Matthews alone made her blurt, "Wait, you guys. I changed my mind. I need you."

"Okay." Christine took a front row seat on the bottom bleacher. Brittany and Marguerite sat next to her.

Dina nodded with a brief smile of thanks and took a deep breath. Coach Matthews stood off to the side of the court talking with Coach Vaughn, the eighth grade coach. Dina walked up to the coaches, stared at the floor, and waited for them to finish their conversation.

Coach Vaughan seemed seriously peeved about something. "I don't see why we can't get a professional indoor volleyball league established here in the United States. Even Iceland has pro teams for heaven's sake."

Coach Matthews nodded in agreement and turned to Dina. "What's up, Stretch?"

Coach Vaughn excused herself to work with one of her eighth grade players.

"Um, I, uh . . ." Out of the corner of her eye, Dina saw her friends pantomime encouragement from their bleacher seats.

"What is it?" Coach Matthews picked up her clipboard from the riser and started to walk toward the PE office.

Dina fell into step. "I have Rosh Hashanah." She felt her face turn red because she knew her coach wouldn't understand. "I mean, on Friday. Rosh Hashanah starts on Friday night."

Coach Matthews stopped walking and turned to Dina. "We play St. Agnes Catholic on Friday night. What are you saying?"

Here it comes. Dina cringed. "I, I can't go to the game. I havta be in Temple." She held her breath and waited. She couldn't look Coach Matthews directly in the eye, so she stared at her coach's shoulder.

"Are you kidding me, Dina Jacobs?" Coach Matthews's voice rose. "Do you know how hard I've worked putting together a championship team? And you're telling me you can't make the game? It would have been nice to get a little more advanced notice."

The entire gym had gotten quiet. Even Coach Vaughn stared at them with a surprised look on her face.

"I'm sorry," Dina squeaked. "I didn't mean it. It's just, I mean I havta . . ." She took a deep breath as she tried to find the right words, but Coach Matthews's glare made that impossible. "It's the start of high-holy days, and I havta go. I don't have a choice."

"We always have a choice, Miss Jacobs. We always have a choice. We'll discuss this later." Coach Matthews stormed away toward the girls' PE office.

Dina slinked back to her friends. Once again she felt the sting of tears in her eyes.

Christine patted her on the back again. "You'll be okay. She'll calm down. I think you just took her by surprise."

"Yeah," Marguerite and Brittany agreed.

Dina smacked the bleacher seat with her open hand. "I could use a side out about now."

"What do you mean?" Christine asked.

"I mean, like, I need to be in control of something for a change. Somebody steals my coins—it's been four weeks—and now Coach Matthews goes all supernova on me." Dina continued to rant as they walked into the locker room. "It's not like I told her I was quitting the team or anything. You know? I havta go to Temple. I can't just skip it. It would be like scheduling a game on Easter Sunday for you guys. Ya know?"

"We get it." Christine stuck out her lower lip. "Right guys?"

"Yeah," Brittany said.

Marguerite patted Dina on the back. "You really do need a side out."

Dina put on the best smile she could for her friends. "Thanks, guys."

"Hey," Christine flicked Dina on the arm with the back of her hand, "I know how we can step up Operation Shakedown. Are you game?"

Dina nodded and managed a cautious smile. She couldn't wait to see what Christine had cooked up. At least it would take her mind off of the supernova she had just ignited.

Chapter 18
Chicago Blackhawks

Mr. Robertson hadn't started the class yet when Christine turned around, placed both elbows on Dina's desk, and rested her head on her fists. "Your parents are meeting with Coach Matthews right now?" Her eyes practically bugged out of her head.

Dina nodded. "In the athletic director's office. My dad was furious when I told him how Coach Matthews had a cow about Friday's game."

"You have to do your Rosh Hashanah thing. What's so hard to understand about that?" Christine shook her head.

"Okay, ladies and gentleman," Mr. Robertson said from behind the lectern. "Will you kindly give your attention to Mr. Benson, please? He has brought in some, er, rather interesting items for his Show-and-Tell project. Ready, Aaron?"

Aaron nodded and walked up to the front of the room, clutching a greasy, rumpled paper bag. Dina could only imagine what was in it. He stepped behind the lectern and set the bag gently on top. The contents settled and sounded like metal that had broken into a million pieces.

Aaron cleared his throat and opened the top of the bag. His face turned fire-engine red all the way to the roots of his blonde crew cut. Dina almost felt sorry for him as the red crept up his face to tint his ears.

"I brought in these." He pulled something out of the bag and held it high for the class to see.

Dina and her classmates laughed at the Budweiser bottle cap.

"Figures the redneck brings in beer caps," Christine whispered just loud enough for Dina to hear.

Dina put a hand over her mouth, so she wouldn't burst out laughing.

"Okay, this one is a Budweiser cap," Aaron continued. "I got all these caps from my Uncle Billy. He likes Budweiser, especially." The class chuckled again, and Aaron smiled. "Well, Budweiser used to be an American beer. Well, okay, it still is kind of, but a company in Belgium bought them. My Uncle Billy was really pissed."

Mr. Robertson cleared his throat loudly.

"Oh, sorry. What I meant to say is that my Uncle Billy was, um, disappointed. Some company named InBev or something like that from Belgium bought them out." Aaron rooted around in the pocket of his cargo pants and pulled out a metal object that looked like a bullet. He pointed the bullet toward the world map on the classroom wall. "This is where Belgium is." A red dot shined on the country. The bullet turned out to be a small laser pointer. "Belgium is in Europe, and it's right next to France, Germany, Netherlands, and," he hesitated for a second, "Lux?"

"Luxembourg," Mr. Robertson said.

"Oh yeah, Luxembourg. Belgium's capital is Brussels, and they have three official languages, which is, like, way weird, but they speak French, German, and Dutch there."

Aaron then upended the bag and spilled the entire contents onto the lectern. "I got a lot more caps here to show you guys."

He searched through the pile, and his eyes lit up when he found the one he was looking for. Dina had a hard time seeing from the back row, but it looked as if the cap had a picture of a Native American on it.

"This is one of the NHL caps that Labatt Brewery put out. Go Blackhawks."

"Yeah," Tyler said and held up his hand with the index and pinky fingers spread out.

Aaron returned the rock and roll gesture and nodded. Apparently, Aaron and Tyler were big Blackhawk ice hockey fans.

"My uncle," Aaron continued, "has almost the whole set, but he's missing three—the Boston Bruins, New Jersey Devils, and the Toronto Maple Leafs. This one is his favorite though." He held the Blackhawks' cap up high like a prized trophy. "Mine, too. Oh, the Labatt Company is from Canada." He used his laser pointer to indicate Canada on the map.

He rooted around in the pile and showed several more of the NHL caps. "Oh, here, let me just pass them around." He scooped up the NHL caps and dumped the whole bunch onto a boy's desk in the front row.

"Okay, this cap is kind of plain, but it's from the Aldaris Brewery in Latvia." He held up a blue cap with the word Aldaris written on it. "See Sweden up there?" He pointed to the map with his laser pointer. "Latvia's right under Sweden on the Baltic Sea. I think Latvia's called a Baltic country or something." He looked back at Mr. Robertson for confirmation. Mr. Robertson nodded. "They speak Latvian, Russian, and German. The capital is called, um . . . oh shoot, I forgot." He looked down at his notes. "Oh, yeah, Ragu. No, no, I mean Riga. Sorry, my mistake. The capital of Latvia is Riga." He sighed in relief, and the class chuckled.

"Okay, Latvia borders Lithuania, Belarus, Russia, and Estonia. Oh, and I have caps from Russia and Estonia, too." He rooted around his pile and pulled out a dozen or so caps which he also dumped on the same boy's desk. "Oh, and those countries used to be a part of the giant Soviet Union until they all broke up."

Mr. Robertson nodded.

The girl in front of Christine passed back a couple of the caps. Christine took them and then turned around to face Dina. She held up the Chicago Blackhawks' cap. Dina thought Christine was going to hand it to her, but instead stashed it in her shirt pocket. Dina widened her eyes. She shook her head slightly to tell Christine she shouldn't steal the cap. Christine ignored her and turned back around.

Dina was horrified that Christine would do the exact same thing that Aaron had done to her. Well, she still wasn't one-hundred percent sure that Aaron had stolen her coins, but still, it wasn't right. Wars got started over stupid things like that, and she wasn't interested in starting a war with somebody in her second month at a new school.

Dina brainstormed ways to convince Christine that two wrongs didn't make a right and that you should do unto others as you'd have them do unto you, but she couldn't say all that without disrupting the class. She started to sweat as Aaron brought his presentation to a close and collected his caps, except for the Blackhawks' cap that was still in Christine's pocket. The class clapped, and Aaron returned to his seat.

Mr. Robertson stood up. "Thank you, Aaron. Personally, I can't stand beer, but I don't think I realized how many countries brewed the foul stuff. I guess I learned something today, too." He laughed, and the class laughed with him. He put his hand up for attention. "I have some great news. Apparently an anonymous good Samaritan has found Dina's lost coins." He held up a small white envelope. He gestured for Dina to come forward to get them. "I'm very pleased that the coins have been found."

Dina was so relieved that her precious coins had turned up, she practically sprinted to Mr. Robertson's desk. Christine's plan to step up Operation Shakedown had obviously worked. Christine had started a rumor that the police were going to fingerprint everybody at Earhart Middle School if the coins didn't show up soon. She had even put black ink on her fingertips to show that she had already had it done, and made sure everybody, including Aaron and Tyler, saw them.

"Thanks, so much," Dina said as she took the envelope. On her way back to her seat, she stared down Christine and tried to telepathically get her to take the bottle cap out of her pocket and give it back to Aaron.

Mr. Robertson outlined their at-home research project based on beer bottle caps when Christine nonchalantly dropped her pen. She bent over as if to get her pen and snuck the bottle cap onto the floor. She then reached out for the fallen pen and also picked up the bottle cap. She sat back up and raised her hand.

"Yes, Christine?" Mr. Robertson said.

She held up the coveted Blackhawks' bottle cap. "This was on the floor."

"Okay, pass it over to Aaron, please."

Christine handed the cap to the girl next to her who handed it to Aaron.

Aaron's expression turned to one of panic when he realized he'd almost lost his uncle's precious Blackhawks' cap. "Thanks." He tossed the Blackhawks' cap into the crumpled paper bag and closed it tight. He blew out a long sigh.

Dina patted Christine on the back to tell her she approved. Christine turned around and nodded. Dina could tell by Christine's flushed cheeks that she was embarrassed by the whole situation.

The bell rang to end the period, and everybody stood up. An office aide came into the classroom and handed a note to Mr. Robertson. He thanked the aide and opened the note. "Dina?"

"Yes?"

"For you." He held the note up for her.

Dina slung her backpack over one shoulder and went up for the note. She opened it slowly.

"What is it?" Christine asked.

"It says that I have to go to the athletic director's office immediately." She and Christine exchanged glances. "Oh, I seriously don't want to see Coach Matthews right now."

"No kidding. She's probably righteously steamed."

Dina took a deep breath and nodded. They stepped into the hallway and headed in opposite directions.

Chapter 19
The Worst Day Ever

Dina held the straps of her backpack so tightly that her hands ached. Dr. Lewiski's office was somewhere down by the gym. She checked each door carefully and almost gave up when she reached the nurse's office at the end of the corridor. She heard her father's laugh come from somewhere around the corner and relaxed the stranglehold on her backpack. If her father was laughing then maybe Coach Matthews wasn't going to kill her after all.

She walked past the nurse's office, turned down a dark corridor, and finally found the athletic director's office. She stood in front of the closed door and took a couple of deep breaths to calm her nerves. Just as she reached out to knock, the late bell rang causing her to jump. Her heart pounded so hard that she had to take another deep breath before knocking.

"C'mon in," a female voice called from inside.

Dina opened the door and relief flooded through her. Coach Matthews wasn't in the room. She was surprised to see Coach Vaughn, the eighth grade coach, there instead. She hugged her parents and then took the seat Dr. Lewiski motioned for her to take.

Dr. Lewiski peered at Dina over her glasses. "You've created quite a stir, young lady."

Dina widened her eyes, and she looked first at her mother and then her father. Her father winked at her and smiled. She had no idea what was going on. Dr. Lewiski gestured toward Coach Vaughn to speak.

"Well, Dina," Coach Vaughn said, "I'm sorry things had to come about this way, but actually we've been thinking about this for a while."

Her mother smiled, making Dina more confused than ever.

"Dina," Coach Vaughn said with a chuckle, "we've decided to move you up to the eighth grade team. Today."

"Are you serious?" Dina felt a little dizzy. "How come?"

"Well," Coach Vaughn continued, "Coach Matthews and I think you'll fit in a lot better skill-wise with the bigger girls. Assuming that's okay with you?"

"More than okay. Thanks, Coach."

Coach Vaughn nodded with a smile.

Dina turned to the athletic director. "Thanks, Dr. Lewiski."

"You're welcome, Dina." Dr. Lewiski held up her Styrofoam coffee cup in salute.

"So, Dina," Coach Vaughn said, "I'll see you on the eighth grade court for practice on Monday."

After the meeting, Dina walked her parents to the school's exit, and then practically skipped to her math class. She had gotten promoted to the eighth grade team. That was seriously cool. She hoped she would fit in with the older kids. Wait 'til she told Christine.

She stopped dead in her tracks just outside the door to her math class. Christine. How was she going to tell her they wouldn't be on the same team anymore?

Brittany pounded the lunch table as she tried to finish her story. She sputtered, "So, so, my mom said to my dad that she wanted to go to India-no-place for dinner, and he drove us to the Bombay Indian restaurant on River Road in West Lafayette."

Christine and Marguerite laughed, but Dina didn't get the joke. She put her hands up to say that she had no clue why it was funny. Her friends laughed even more.

Christine finally caught her breath. "India-no-place means Indianapolis. The capital of Indiana."

"Oh," Dina said with a chuckle. "I get it. India-no-place. That's kinda funny."

"Are you going to eat your pretzels?" Christine hovered her hand over Dina's small bag.

"Oh, no. Go ahead." Dina pushed the unopened bag of pretzels across the table toward Christine.

"Hey, you're kind of quiet, today, Dina," Marguerite said. "Are you okay?"

"Yeah, yeah." Dina tried to look cool and collected, but she held the weight of the world on her shoulders. She had to tell them about Coach Vaughn's decision to move her up to the eighth grade team, but she didn't know how.

She was just about to break the news in the noisy lunchroom when Aaron Benson walked up to their table and stood next to her.

"Dina?" he said.

"Hey, Aaron. What's up?" As she turned her head to look at him, she caught the glare Christine shot him. He must have seen it, too, because his face turned crimson. Dina tried not to smile at his obvious unease, but she thought it served him right for stealing her coins.

"I, uh, I wanted to say I'm glad you got your coins back." He broke eye contact with her to look at the floor.

"Thanks," Dina said. "I'm glad I got them back, too. They're kind of special because my dad traveled all that way to Japan and Israel to get them."

"I know. I know. I'm sorry."

Aha, Dina thought, *he's admitting that he took them.*

"I kind of know how you felt, 'cuz if I hadda gone home without that Blackhawks' bottle cap, my uncle woulda strapped me for sure." His words came out in a jumbled mess.

Dina swallowed hard. Her mother always told her that apologizing was one of the hardest things a person could do. And here was Aaron standing in front of her, not exactly admitting he stole the coins, but apologizing nonetheless. Her mom said if someone gave you a sincere apology you should put aside your differences, accept the apology, and move on from there.

Dina decided that since she had her coins back, and Aaron had his precious Blackhawks' bottle cap back that she would go ahead and let Aaron off the hook. "Hey, ya know what? It's no biggie. Seriously, okay? We're good." She held out her fist.

"Really?" The relieved smile that burst from his face almost made Dina laugh. He gently tapped her fist with his. "Cool. Okay, I'll see you around." He spun on his heels and went back to the table he shared with Tyler and his other friends.

"Okay," Brittany said. "That was weird."

Dina shrugged. "You guys? I have some good news. Well, it's good news that's kind of bad news, too." Before anyone had a chance to ask, she blurted, "Coach Vaughn moved me up to the eighth grade team."

"That's awesome," Marguerite said. "You really deserve it."

"Take us with you," Brittany begged. "Don't leave us alone with Coach Matthews." She pretended to sob into her sweatshirt, and Marguerite pretended to console her.

Dina would have laughed at their silliness, except that Christine looked like she was about to cry.

"Christine . . ." Dina started, but wasn't quite sure what to say. "I'm sorry." She wasn't sure why she was apologizing, but it felt like the right thing to do.

Christine bolted from her chair, knocking it over, and ran toward the girls' bathroom.

"Christine, I didn't mean it. It wasn't my fault," Dina called after her. She stood up and looked at Marguerite and Brittany. "Should I go after her?"

Marguerite shook her head. "No, give her some time. She has to get used to the idea."

"And, besides," Brittany added, "you guys can talk at the game later." As if realizing her mistake she groaned. "Oh, yeah. Sorry. You're not on our team anymore."

Dina sat down hard on the plastic chair. "I won't be at the eighth grade game either. I'm going home right after school for Rosh Hashanah."

Marguerite nodded. "Maybe you should go talk to her now then."

The bell rang to end the lunch period. Dina groaned and stood up. "Crap. I'll just call her later."

The day that had started out so good, had just turned into the worst day ever.

Chapter 20
Rosh Hashanah

Rosh Hashanah was supposed to be a celebration. It was the Jewish New Year, after all, but Dina couldn't find much enthusiasm for the holiday. She lay on her bed, staring at the ceiling, her stomach stuffed with the feast her mother had made for them—honey glazed chicken and challah bread dipped in honey. Everything was sweet to symbolize the hope for a sweet new year, but as much as she tried, she couldn't quite capture the feeling. All she could think about was seeing Christine running out of the cafeteria upset. The scene played over and over in her mind.

Dina slapped her bedspread. She should have run after Christine right away. She tried to talk to her after school, but Christine didn't have time. She had to change into her uniform and get on the bus for the game at St. Agnes Catholic School.

Dina stared at the ceiling some more and then glanced at her cell phone on the bedside stand. She wasn't sure if she should call Christine or not. She should be home from the game by now. She wondered how the team had played, and if Coach Matthews was still mad at her.

She sat up, grabbed the phone, and stared at it hard. She willed Christine to call her, but when the phone didn't miraculously ring after an entire minute, she looked away with a sigh. Maybe Robyn could tell her what to do. She hit the voice dial button.

"*Schmeggegy,*" she said into her phone, and it dialed Robyn's cell phone on Long Island. She couldn't remember if New York and Indiana were in the same time zone. She hoped that Robyn wasn't still having dinner with her family.

Dina groaned in frustration when Robyn's voice mail picked up.

"*L'Shanah Tovah, Schmegeggy.* Happy New Year. It's me, your favorite *meshugana* in Indiana." Dina desperately wanted Robyn's help, but she didn't know how to leave a message that said she'd messed up everything with her new best friend in Indiana. She sighed. "Don't fall asleep in Temple tomorrow. Ha ha. Okay, see ya. I mean *talk* to ya later."

Dina tossed the phone toward the foot of her bed, got up, and sat on the floor. With a grunt she turned over and lay face down on the soft Berber carpet. She put her hands out near her shoulders and pushed up. Fifty pushups later she still wasn't sure if she should call Christine or not. One hundred sit-ups later, she decided she should, because she didn't want to do jumping jacks.

She leaped off the floor, grabbed her cell phone from the bottom of the bed, and sat down. She hadn't quite caught her breath, so she held on to the phone for a while longer. She'd tell Christine it wasn't her idea or even her parents' idea to get moved up. It was Coach Vaughn's.

Dina took a deep breath for courage and jumped when the phone rang in her hand. With her heart pounding, she looked at the caller ID expecting it to read, "Robyn." To her amazement, it read, "Christine."

She hit the answer button. "Hey."

"Hey," Christine said. "Is your Rosh Hashanah over?"

Dina desperately wanted to talk about volleyball and all that stuff right away, but maybe it'd be better to wait. At least Christine was talking to her again. "Not really. My dad went to Temple tonight, but we'll all go tomorrow. He said the tickets weren't as expensive here in Indiana like they are in New York."

"Tickets? You have to buy tickets to go to church? Oh, sorry. I meant Temple."

"Yeah, Rosh Hashanah starts the high holy days, so services are really popular. Some people only go to Temple for Rosh Hashanah and Yom Kippur. My dad calls them twice-a-year Jews."

"That's funny." Christine laughed. "We have twice-a-year

Catholics, too. Christmas and Easter. The church is always packed on those days. Don't tell Father Walters about that ticket thing, though. He might start charging us."

Dina laughed. "Okay, I won't."

She listened to Christine's breathing as an awkward silence grew between them.

She cleared her throat. "So, how did the game go?"

"We got spanked."

"You did? Did Brittany get any good sets?"

"Yeah, she was fine, but I couldn't do anything." Christine grunted. "None of my serves would go over, and the few that actually did go over got set up for kills, so they got the points anyway."

"Sorry."

"It's okay. Marguerite played good."

"Cool. How was Coach Matthews?" Dina held her breath, waiting for the answer.

"Fine, actually. She was calmer than ever." Christine chuckled. "Scary calm. I think maybe she got in trouble for yelling at you."

"Seriously?"

"Yeah, because she didn't yell at anybody. Even when we had, like, five service errors in a row."

"I hope she doesn't take it out on you guys at practice on Monday." Dina lay down on her bed and stared at the ceiling without seeing it. "I feel bad."

"Don't feel bad. I'm sorry I freaked at lunch today."

"I didn't know how to tell you." Dina sighed. "It's not like I asked to be moved. Seriously, I'd rather stay with you guys."

"Oh, no you don't." Christine's voice was stern.

"Why not?"

"Don't say you want to stay back with us. I've been thinking about it, and you really deserve to be moved up. You were the best player on our team. Better than everybody else—"

"No, I'm—"

"Shuddup. Yes, you are. First of all you're five foot freakin' nine. You can jump higher than anybody, and most of your kills actually make it over the net. Only half of Marguerite's go over. Coach Matthews should have moved you up right away."

"I don't know." Dina felt her face get warm at Christine's praise.

"I can't wait to see you in spandex shorts." Christine laughed into the phone.

Dina sat bolt upright. "Oh, shoot. I forgot about the spandex. Don't laugh at me, okay?"

"I won't. You're practicing with them on Monday, right?"

"Yeah," Dina said, "and then my first game with them is Wednesday against Kickapoo."

"So, I guess I'll see you in the gym then."

"Christine?"

"Yeah?"

"We're, like, still friends, right? I mean . . ." Dina didn't want to lose her friend just because they couldn't share the thing that had brought them together.

"Of course we are. We still have Mr. Robertson's Social Studies Zone, and we'll still eat lunch together, right?"

"Yeah." Dina felt her shoulders relax a little, even though they were sore from all the pushups. "And maybe we can go to a few more Purdue volleyball games."

"Absolutely. Oh, that reminds me, Purdue plays Michigan State next Friday. Is your Rosh Hashanah over by then?"

"Yeah, it's over, but then we have Yom Kippur. That doesn't start until sundown next Sunday, so I should be good to go."

"Cool. I'll ask my mom. Michigan State's ranked, like, sixteenth in the whole country."

"Seriously? What's Purdue ranked again?"

"Purdue was ranked nineteenth at one point, but not now. I'm not sure what they're ranked, but it's not in the top twenty-five."

"Hmm," Dina said, "I guess we need to go and change their luck. Can we go to the Triple XXX again?"

"You feel the need for peanut butter on your hamburger?" Christine teased.

"I don't know. Maybe."

"For real?"

"Why not?" Dina shrugged, even though Christine couldn't see her through the phone. "My dad says he tries new food all the time."

"Okay, if you will then I will."

They chatted away about the Triple XXX and their favorite Purdue volleyball players until her mother knocked on her bedroom door.

"Dina?"

"Hang on, Christine." Dina put the phone down against her chest. "C'mon in."

Her mother opened the door a crack and peeked in. "Come say goodnight to Daddy. He's back from Temple and would like to go to bed."

"Okay, Mom. I'll be out in a second. I just have to hang up with Christine."

"You should be getting ready for bed, too. We all have a big day tomorrow."

Dina nodded, and then her mother closed the door as she left the room.

"Christine?"

"Yeah?"

"I have to go, but I'll see you in school on Monday."

"Do you want to come over on Sunday?"

"Oh, I can't. I have to go to Temple on Sunday, too."

"Two days in a row?" Christine sounded amazed.

"Some people go every day."

"Yeah, you're right. Some Catholics go to church every day, too."

"I actually want to go on Sunday. Rosh Hashanah falls on Saturday this year and you can't blow the shofar on Saturday. They'll blow it on Sunday."

"Oh, that's that ram's horn thing you were telling me about?"

"Yeah, they blow it to wake us up, like, not literally, but in spirit. To wake us up to the new year, so we can think about how we're going to take responsibility for our thoughts and actions."

"Sounds heavy." Christine laughed. "My church puts that heavy guilt trip on us, too, sometimes. All religions do that, don't they?"

"Yeah, seriously," Dina agreed. "Okay, I really gotta go now. Happy New Year."

Christine laughed. "Okay, it's only September, but Happy New Year to you, too. See you Monday."

Dina hung up her cell phone and smiled. At least everything seemed to be okay with Christine. Monday's eighth grade team practice might be another story, though. She leaped off the bed, threw open the door, and raced to say goodnight to her parents.

Chapter 21
New Beginnings

Dina and Christine made their way out of the locker room and onto the practice court.

"I guess I leave you here," Dina said. She looked at her soon-to-be new teammates warming up on the eighth grade court.

Christine followed Dina's gaze. "Are you nervous?"

"Yeah, kind of. Look at 'em." She gestured toward the bigger girls and grimaced for effect. "They're so, I dunno, serious about volleyball."

Christine nodded. "Yeah, they are. They only have one loss, I think. Coach Matthews wants us to act like them. All business."

"She makes it feel like we're in the Army."

Christine laughed, but then turned serious when Coach Matthews called for the seventh grade team to circle up. "Gotta go. I'll see you after practice. Good luck."

"Thanks. See ya."

Dina checked her ponytail to make sure it was securely tacked to her head and sauntered over to her new teammates. She tried to act cool, like she belonged. The eighth graders were digging and setting the ball back and forth. She stood off to the side and stretched.

An Asian girl caught the ball her partner bumped to her and faced Dina. "Are you the new kid?"

Dina felt her face flush. "Yeah." She hoped the girl would think her red cheeks were from the warm gym. "I'm Dina." She started to stick her hand out in handshake, but pulled it back at the last second. Christine had told her that they didn't do that kind of thing in Indiana, that it had been weird when Dina shook her hand the first time they met. It must be a New York thing. She kept her hand anchored to her side.

"Nice to meet you, Dina. I'm Mikiko, but everybody calls me Miki. This is Stephanie." She indicated the tall blonde girl she had been warming up with.

"Hey," Stephanie said with a nod.

Dina nodded back. "Nice to meet you guys." She stretched her quads as they talked.

Miki tossed the ball back to Stephanie. "Coach Vaughn told us you'd been moved up."

"Yeah." She didn't want to tell her new teammates that she and Coach Matthews didn't get along. "I can't wait to play."

"Kickapoo on Wednesday," Stephanie said, her long blonde braid swinging as she stretched next to Dina. "Coach said their team is really good."

"But we're better, right?" Miki grinned at Stephanie.

"Here's hoping."

Coach Vaughn blew her whistle. "Bring it in girls."

Dina stood with Miki on one side in the loosely formed circle and a tall girl with shoulder-length curly hair on the other. Her nerves jangled. This was another new beginning. There had been so many new things in such a short time—the move to Indiana, the new house, the new Temple, her new school and teachers and classmates, the seventh grade team, and now the latest new thing—the eighth grade team.

Dina jumped up and down in place a few times, trying to get her nerves under control.

Coach Vaughn looked up from her clipboard. "After your laps, we're going to work on our plays. Dina doesn't know any of them, and with a game in two days, let's hope she's a quick study."

Dina smiled when the team laughed good-naturedly. Miki patted her on the back. "Stick with me, kid, and you'll be okay."

"Okay." Dina grinned. Maybe moving up wouldn't be so hard after all.

Coach Vaughn outlined the rest of their practice which seemed to involve seven thousand drills and even more sprints and laps. After their warm up laps, Coach Vaughn climbed onto the official's riser. The bin of balls sat conveniently below her, and Lori, an eighth grade girl who was the team's manager, stood ready to hand the balls up to her.

"Starting lineup, take your positions," Coach Vaughn called. "Non-starters you know who you go in for. You'll go in once we've made one complete circuit, but for now go to the other side of the court and dig every kill back up. Rotate so you all take a turn digging, chasing loose balls, and putting the balls into the bin."

Dina nodded and headed to the other side of the court. Three of the non-starters had already claimed digging duty, so she ended up with the least desirable job of chasing down the loose balls.

Miki headed onto the floor into the setter's usual starting position, and Stephanie lined up in the outside hitter's spot. Dina's heart sank. That was her position. There was no way she'd ever play with Stephanie there. Even though they were about the same height, Stephanie was a lot better. Dina shuffled her feet on the sidelines, ready to be the best ball retriever on the planet.

"Oh, Dina," Coach Vaughn called. "You'll be subbing in for Grace at middle blocker, okay?" Grace was the girl with the shoulder-length curly hair.

"Okay." Dina was surprised. She hadn't ever thought about playing middle, but maybe it would be okay because that's what Kristen Arthurs played for Purdue.

Coach Vaughn called the play and threw the ball down hard at the back row. Zola, a dark-skinned girl with a small fro, passed the ball to Miki who set it up for Stephanie. Stephanie leaped into the air and, with a sharp snap of her wrist, sent the ball rocketing to the floor. One of the girls dove for it, but was way too late.

Dina's heart pounded. She was glad she hadn't been on the receiving end of Stephanie's kill.

"Nice kill, Stephanie," Coach Vaughn called, but sent another ball to the back row before they had a chance to regroup.

Zola dove for the ball and sent it to Miki. This time Miki back set to Grace, the team's middle hitter. Grace leaped high and hit the ball. The ball hit the tape on top of the net and didn't go over. Miki scrambled but couldn't get to it. She smacked a fist against her thigh as it bounced away. Grace rubbed her wrist.

Coach Vaughn hopped down from the riser and headed onto the court. "Here, Grace, let me see." She felt all around the wrist. "Is it still sore from Friday's game?"

Grace nodded.

"It feels all right, but let's get an ice pack on it and have you see the trainer after practice, okay?"

Grace nodded. "Sorry, Coach."

"No, don't worry about it. You're hurt, and we have to baby that wrist. If we push you too hard now you may not be able to play against Kickapoo on Wednesday."

Lori, the manager, had already gone to the medical kit and held out an ice pack for Grace. Grace flopped onto the team bench, looking not very happy about having to sit out.

And Dina knew why.

"Dina," Coach Vaughn called. "Looks like you're in sooner than expected." She gestured to the spot on the floor that Grace had just vacated. She turned toward Miki. "Help her with your signals, so she knows what's going on, okay?"

Miki nodded and turned to Dina who was trying to get her heart to stop pounding so she could hear her new teammate. "This next one's coming to you high on a back set. The next one'll probably be for you, too, but with a short set." She smiled as if to reassure Dina.

Dina smiled back. "Okay."

"Ready, girls?" Coach Vaughn called, ball in hand.

Miki, obviously the floor leader, said, "Bring it on, Coach."

Coach Vaughn laughed. "Okay, you asked for it." She threw the ball down hard. Zola bumped it up to Miki who, as promised, sent a back set to Dina.

Dina wasn't used to hitting the ball from the middle blocker's position, but she took her steps, leaped up, and put all her power into her kill. The ball sizzled over the net and smashed untouched onto the floor.

A cheer went up from her teammates.

"Way to go, Stretch." Miki clapped her on the back.

"Nice job, Newbie," Stephanie called over.

"Thanks." Dina took a deep breath. Her heart was still pounding, and the short set was next.

Coach Vaughn threw the ball down to the back row. A short girl with braces dug it up to Miki. Miki got under it and back set the ball, but short. Dina didn't have to time to think because she was already in motion. She successfully hit the ball over the net, but without as much power as her first hit. Hits from the short set were definitely something she'd have to practice.

"Way to go, Dina," Christine called from the seventh grade practice. "You go, New Yawker."

Dina shot her a grin, then quickly turned back to her own practice. She only had two short practices to prove to Coach Vaughn and her new teammates that she belonged there. She felt really good about her first two kills, until she turned to see Grace glaring at her from the sidelines.

Chapter 22
Kickapoo

The eighth grade team stood in a circle on their home court and put their arms around each other. Stephanie Andrews, the team's outside hitter, was on one side of Dina, her long blonde braid tickling her forearm, and Zola D'Anifrue, the libero, stood on the other.

Stephanie started the circle swaying from side to side. "We have heart."

"We have strength," Bernadette, the player on the other side of Stephanie, said.

The circle swayed with more intensity as each girl spoke words of encouragement. Dina still hadn't come up with anything to say when Zola's turn came up.

"We are brilliant," Zola said.

In a flash, Dina remembered her father saying, "We have hope for a sweet new year," during their Rosh Hashanah dinner, so she said, "We have hope."

"Good one, Stretch." Stephanie patted her shoulder. "Ready?" she called out to her teammates.

"Ready," the team answered in unison.

"One-two-three," Stephanie yelled. "Goooooo Flyers. Whoooo!" They untangled themselves, and Stephanie clapped Dina on the back with a laugh. "That was a good one. I didn't know what you'd come up with."

"Thanks." Dina felt herself blushing and looked away. She sat on the team bench and smoothed out her new uniform shirt. She was disappointed that Stephanie wore Logan Tom's number fifteen, but Dina had been able to snag Kristen Andrew's number sixteen instead. She was also a little self-conscious about the spandex shorts, but they felt kind of freeing, so maybe it wouldn't be too bad. She just hoped no one would make fun of her for wearing them.

Dina was a bench warmer. Before the game, Coach had told her she couldn't make any promises about getting her in the game, so she sat at the end of the bench next to one of the other girls who hardly ever played.

Both teams' starting lineups were called. Her new teammates took their positions on the court, and the game began. Dina looked up and found her parents in the bleachers. Her dad cheered at the action, while her mom sat quietly watching the ball go back and forth over the net.

Her mom wasn't into sports that much, and yet always sat patiently through all of Dina's school and club team games. Her dad, on the other hand, loved all sports. He always said he loved two teams—the New York Yankees and whatever team Dina was playing on. She wished Christine was in the stands, but she had an away game. It stunk that they played on different teams now.

Dina's attention was drawn back to the court as a particularly long volley ended with a point for Kickapoo tying up the score 2-2.

"That's all right. You'll get the next one," Coach Vaughn called out.

Miki flashed the signal for a high set to Grace. Dina watched with interest, because if Coach Vaughn subbed her in later, she would sub in for Grace. The serve from the Kickapoo side of the court floated across the net. Zola got under the ball easily and passed it up to Miki. Miki set the ball high, and Grace launched herself at it. She snapped her wrist, and the ball floated weakly over the net. A Kickapoo player got under the hit easily and passed the ball to their setter who set it up for their outside hitter. Grace and Stephanie smacked hips as they leaped up to block the Kickapoo hit. The smash knocked Grace's hand back, and she cried out in pain. The ball trickled down off the net and hit the floor for another Kickapoo point making the score 2-3 in their favor.

"Time out," Coach Vaughn yelled. Grace clutched her wrist to her chest.

Dina cringed at the obvious pain on Grace's face and the tears she was trying to keep under control.

"Dina," Coach Vaughn summoned.

Dina leaped off the folding chair and hurried over to the coach.

"You're subbing in for Grace."

Dina took a deep breath to calm her nerves and waited for the up official to write the substitution on her little card. Once finished, she waved them through.

"I hope you're okay," Dina whispered to Grace as she went by.

"Thanks." Grace's eyes filled with tears. She sat on the chair Dina had just vacated and put an ice pack on her wrist.

Dina stepped onto the court for the first time in her first official game with the eighth grade team.

Miki pulled Dina into a quick team circle. "We're going to you first thing, Stretch. They have no idea that you're our secret weapon."

"Okay." Dina felt her cheeks get warm. She hoped she could keep up with the eighth graders. They were all so much bigger and stronger than the girls she was used to playing with.

She took her spot on the floor. The Kickapoo serve came hard over the net, but Zola passed it up to Miki. Dina's stomach tingled as she approached Miki's sweet set. She leaped, swung her arm, and followed through with a quick wrist snap. The ball zinged to the floor. Point Flyers.

Her teammates surrounded her in an instant.

"I guess they know about our secret weapon now," Miki said, and her teammates laughed.

"Time out," the Kickapoo Coach called to the up official on the riser. The official blew her whistle, and the Flyers huddled near the sideline for the time-out.

Coach Vaughn hustled over. "Looks like they're on to Dina already. So let's keep them guessing." She turned to Miki. "Keep changing up the sets, front and back, high and low. Go back to Stephanie and Bernadette for a while, but then get Dina back in the loop for some hits."

Miki nodded.

Coach Vaughn turned to Dina. "I want you to focus on blocking right now. Your role on the seventh grade team was hitting, but you have to change your focus a bit. Think about blocking as your number one job, okay?"

Dina nodded.

"Go get 'em," Coach Vaughn said as the official blew her whistle to end the time-out.

Bernadette, the Flyers weak-side hitter, served the ball over the net. The Kickapoo back row successfully passed the ball to their setter. Both their strong-side and middle hitters approached. Dina wasn't sure how, but she knew the middle hitter was getting the set.

Dina felt Stephanie right beside her, and together they leaped at just the right moment. The ball bounced against Dina's outstretched hands and then landed on the Kickapoo side of the court for another Flyers' point, giving them a 4-3 lead.

Stephanie high-fived Dina, and they ran to the quick team huddle in the middle of the court. "Nice job, Stretch." They trotted back to their positions. "How'd you know it'd be the middle hitter?"

Dina shrugged. "I dunno."

As the game progressed, Dina got tingles in her stomach whenever she read the Kickapoo's offense. She knew which player was going to attack almost every single time. She got her fair share of kills as well, but adding blocks to her responsibilities made the game so much more exciting.

The final whistle blew, and the Amelia Earhart Middle School Flyers had beaten the Kickapoo Eagles in two straight sets.

Miki patted Dina on the back. "You're a game player. That's for sure. I didn't know you were that good."

"Thanks." Dina followed Miki as they low-fived the Kickapoo team under the net.

"We're seven and one, women," Stephanie said, as they made their way back to Coach Vaughn. "That Star City team better start practicing, 'cuz we're going to kick their bootay in the tournament."

Her teammates sent up a cheer.

Coach Vaughn stuck her hand out to Dina. "Nice job, Dina."

Dina shook the offered hand. "Thanks." She made a mental note to tell Christine that some people in Indiana actually did shake hands.

Coach Vaughn pointed out the good things they did during the game, but then went over some of the things they needed to work on. Dina's elation drained out of her when Coach Vaughn added, "Grace is going for an x-ray tomorrow for her wrist. Hopefully, she's only sidelined temporarily." She flashed a tight-lipped smile at Grace, and the team grew quiet.

Grace started crying softly, and Dina's heart squeezed tight. She had fallen in love with the middle blocker role, but she didn't ever want to take somebody else's position. She instantly felt bad for playing so well.

A different kind of misery took hold when Coach Vaughn said, "We have a big game against Nicolet on Monday. They have one loss, and we have one loss." She grinned. "But we're going to change that on Monday."

The team cheered, but Dina groaned. Monday was Yom Kippur.

Chapter 23
Ramadan

Mr. Robertson stood up from behind his desk as the bell rang to start class.

"I'll explain it you later," Dina whispered to Christine.

"Okay." Christine turned back around in her seat.

Christine had asked her about the difference between Rosh Hashanah and Yom Kippur.

Mr. Robertson stepped behind his lectern, and the students stopped their conversations. "Okay, everybody, for Show-and-Tell today, Mahira is going to give us her insights into India, Islam, and Ramadan." He turned toward the nerdy dark-haired girl in the front row. "All set?"

Mahira nodded and gathered her note cards together. She was the girl in the class who raised her hand constantly and asked a thousand questions. She stood up, and Dina's breath caught at the sight of the nerdy girl transformed.

Although she still wore her glasses, Mahira also had on a sari, a traditional Indian outfit for women. The vibrant yellow and deep red fabric was wrapped around her like a giant silk scarf. One end was draped over her left shoulder, and Dina had no idea how she kept the sari in place, because it didn't seem fastened together in any particular way. Mahira's long dark hair, usually pulled back in a pony tail, was tacked neatly behind her head in a tight bun. She moved gracefully and set her stack of note cards on top of the lectern, her colorful bracelets jangling as she did so.

Mahira shuffled her feet and then coughed into her fist causing the bracelets to jangle again. Her cheeks were bright red, almost matching the red in her sari. She gripped both sides of the lectern, and Dina hoped the girl wouldn't pass out from nerves. Public speaking seemed to bring out the jitters in everyone, and it was weird seeing the class nerd this nervous.

Mahira finally seemed to get her composure and said, "I'm going to tell you all about India today. There are several religions represented in India, Hinduism is the most prevalent, but Islam—that's my religion—is also practiced by a lot of people. I want to tell you about Ramadan, our ritual month of fasting."

Fasting. Dina sat up and paid attention. Every religion seemed to have some kind of self-deprivation ritual built in.

"My Show-and Tell object is this." Mahira stepped out from behind the lectern and waved her arm in front of her outfit. "This is a sari, traditional Indian dress. Oh, that's India Indian, not Native American Indian."

The class laughed politely, and Mahira chuckled with them, which seemed to settle her nerves even more.

"There are lots of ways to wear the sari, but I like to wear it wrapped around my waist and then draped from the front to the back over my left shoulder and pinned in the back. Legend has it that long ago a weaver was daydreaming about the woman he loved and forgot to stop the loom. He ended up with a large piece of cloth with so much love woven into it that it became the most beautiful fabric in all of India. This is the fabric, supposedly, that's used to make saris."

She stepped back behind the lectern. "My parents were born in India, but moved to New York City to go to college. That's where they met. Both my sets of grandparents lived most of their lives in Agra, India." She used Mr. Robertson's laser to point to the city of Agra on the map. "Agra is just outside of New Delhi, the capital. Actually, you may have heard of Agra, because that's where the Taj Mahal is."

Christine whipped her head around to look at Dina. "We're going there," she whispered. "You and me."

Dina nodded, and Christine turned back to face the front of the room.

Dina wanted to ask Mahira if she'd ever been to the Taj Mahal. She'd ask, if there was time at the end of the period. If not then she'd ask on Monday.

Oops, she couldn't ask on Monday, because that was Yom Kippur. She squirmed in her seat because it was already Friday, and she hadn't told Coach Vaughn yet about having to miss Monday's big Nicolet game. She imagined Coach Vaughn hitting the roof harder than Coach Matthews had. Or even worse. Maybe Coach Vaughn would do the exact opposite. Maybe she'd get seriously quiet and tell her how disappointed she was and then demote her back to the seventh grade team. She looked down at her hands on the desk and felt guilty about letting her new team down.

She listened intently when Mahira started talking about fasting and Ramadan.

"Ramadan is the time of year that the Lord wants us to fast. We fast to increase spiritual awareness and to help us get over our faults like greed and selfishness."

Dina couldn't believe what she was hearing. That's exactly what Yom Kippur was all about—a day of fasting to atone for transgressions against G-d, a day to become self-aware.

Mahira's voice was confident and strong, all traces of her nerves gone. "Ramadan doesn't fall on the same date every year because the religion of Islam follows the lunar calendar."

Dina realized that being Jewish didn't make her so different than everybody else in Indiana after all, because Jewish holidays followed the lunar calendar, too. Maybe way back in history, religions started from the same place, but developed different personalities as time and history went on. She decided to ask her mom and dad about it when she got home.

"We fast every single day during Ramadan," Mahira continued, "from sun up to sun down, for an entire month."

Dina blew out a low whistle, meant for only Christine to hear. Christine looked over her shoulder, eyebrows raised, as if to say she couldn't believe they fasted for that long either.

Mahira put up a finger to make an important point. "Fasting doesn't just mean we can't eat. We're not supposed to drink anything either."

"Just like on Yom Kippur," Dina said under her breath.

"Fasting is hard," Mahira continued. "Ramadan began in late August this year, right when school started, but I fasted anyway. I went every single day without eating or drinking, which was really hard at school."

Dina felt like an instant wimp. *All* she had to do for Yom Kippur was fast for one stupid day, but Mahira had fasted for, like, thirty whole days. She firmly decided to do it, no matter how hard it was. The harder part was telling Coach Vaughn she wouldn't be at the volleyball game. She groaned. Why did all her thoughts have to wind up back at having to let down her coach and teammates?

Mahira wrapped up her presentation and then sat down in her usual front row seat. Mr. Robertson stood up. "Great job, Mahira." He started clapping, and the students joined him. He paused for a moment and then looked over the class. "Unfortunately, we don't have time to ask Mahira questions, but she brought up some interesting facts about Islam. What do you think the importance of fasting is?"

Several students raised their hands, but Dina knew she had to be ready to answer the question. Mr. Robertson was tricky because he sometimes called on kids that didn't have their hands raised.

"Dina."

Dina groaned. "Uh, well. It's like G-d asks for a real sacrifice from you. He wants you to fast, so you can focus on Him, and not your earthly pleasures." She felt her cheeks turn warm.

"Good summary," Mr. Robertson said with a wink. He must have remembered that she wouldn't be in class on Monday because of Yom Kippur. "Islam, like Judaism and Christian religions are all monotheistic. What does monotheistic mean?" He looked over the class.

Dina knew what the word meant, but let the other usual kids, including Mahira, raise their hands.

"Aaron?"

Dina chuckled. Aaron hadn't had his hand raised either.

"Uhhh," Aaron stalled. "I don't know. My uncle had mono

last year." A few of the students chuckled. "No, he really did. He was so sick. I wasn't allowed to go over."

"Okay, everybody," Mr. Robertson said, "let's settle down. It's okay not to know something. That's how we learn, right?" He gave Aaron a reassuring smile. "Mono means one, theistic means a supreme being, so monotheistic means of one supreme being. Some religions worship more than one supreme being, and that's called polytheism. Many modern religions are polytheistic."

Dina opened her notebook and uncapped her pen. She knew Mr. Robertson was about to give them their weekend Show-and-Tell assignment.

"The people of India observe several different religions just like in America," Mr. Robertson continued, "so what I'd like you to do is research the polytheistic religion of India called Hinduism. I'd like you to report on a few of the supreme beings they worship."

Dina shut her notebook.

"As usual, one page and cite your sources. All your sources." Mr. Robertson looked up at the clock. "There's only one minute before the bell. Go ahead and pack up."

Christine turned to Dina. "If we get out of practice early enough, my mom said we can go to the Triple XXX again before the Purdue game tonight."

"Really? I'm feeling the need for peanut butter."

"Yeah?" Christine's eyes grew wide.

"Maybe. We'll see." Dina waggled her eyebrows.

The bell rang, and Dina stood up, threw her backpack over one shoulder, and headed toward the door. She almost wished Coach Vaughn had seen Mahira's presentation about Ramadan and the importance of fasting. It would have made explaining Yom Kippur to her a thousand times easier.

Chapter 24
Purdue vs. #16 Michigan State

Dina sat back down in her seat in the packed Purdue gymnasium. Purdue had just won the second set from the Michigan State Spartans and were up two sets to none. Both teams had gone into their respective locker rooms for a brief intermission before the third set. Christine told her this game was the start of play in the Big Ten Conference. No wonder the crazy Purdue students seemed noisier than ever.

"I can't believe we took the first two sets from them." Dina looked at Christine next to her. "One more, and we win."

"I know. Michigan State's undefeated, and they're ranked, like, number sixteen in the country."

"Purdue's not in the top twenty-five anymore, right?"

"Nope." Christine shook her head. "Not since late August or something."

Dina held out her fist. "Ha ha. We're beating a ranked team." Christine bumped Dina's fist in celebration.

Mrs. Hannigan leaned over Joey who sat between her and Christine. "Dina, I love your black Purdue t-shirt. It's flattering with your dark hair."

"Oh, thanks, Mrs. Hannigan. My mom brought it home from work yesterday, so I could wear it tonight."

Joey kicked the seat in front of him. The teenage girl in the seat glanced over her shoulder, but didn't say anything.

Mrs. Hannigan sighed. "He's getting antsy. I think I'll take him outside and run him around a bit."

"Okay, Mom," Christine said. "Hey, are you stopping at the concession stand on the way back?"

"Oh, to be twelve again," her mother said with a laugh. "You're still hungry? Peanut butter hamburgers at the Triple XXX weren't enough?"

"I'm still full." Dina patted her stomach.

"Can you bring us a couple of waters?" Christine sported a toothy grin. "Please?"

"Oh, how can I resist such charm?" Her mother rolled her eyes. "We'll be back in a little while."

"Wait, Mom, can we come back here on Sunday? Purdue plays Michigan."

"Maybe. Let me talk to your father first."

"Okay."

Mrs. Hannigan and Joey made their way out of the row and down the aisle toward the gym exits.

Christine looked at Dina. "Michigan's ranked eighth in the country."

"Eighth? Wow." Dina was stoked. The only college volleyball games she'd ever been to back home were the two Suffolk Community College games she'd gone to with Robyn. Those games were nothing compared to watching Division I Purdue play in a big arena. Christine knew so much about the Big Ten Conference and the NCAA tournament and everything. Dina felt like she had an insider helping her catch up.

"How was your practice today?" Christine asked. "It looked like Coach Vaughn was killing you guys."

"Actually, she makes it kind of fun, so we don't know she's killing us. She changes things up. Coach Matthews always does the same drills over and over. That gets boring after a while."

"Tell me about it. So are you playing middle blocker all the time now?"

"Yeah, it's awesome. You get to be part of almost every play. I always thought blocking was boring."

Christine laughed. "Nothing about volleyball's boring."

"True that."

Christine smacked Dina on the arm. "Ooh, here they come." She pointed to the Purdue team funneling out of their time-out area.

"Fingers crossed." Dina crossed both sets of fingers on each hand.

"Just until we score, okay?" Christine bugged out her eyes. "I can't keep them crossed for the whole game."

"Okay, but you have to cross both sets of fingers on each hand."

"Deal."

After a few minutes, Purdue and Michigan State took their positions on the court for the third set. Purdue served first. Dina groaned when a quick kill by a Michigan State player put them up by a score of 0-1.

"C'mon Boilermakers," she yelled and waved her hands with all the fingers crossed.

Christine gritted her teeth and growled.

Dina widened her eyes. "You scared me with that face."

Christine laughed evilly.

Purdue's powerhouse hitter, Carrie Gurnell, ripped the ball over the net to tie up the score. A cheer went up in the crowd, and with relief, Dina uncrossed all of her fingers and shook them out.

"Thank goodness," Christine said. "My fingers were getting tired."

"Seriously."

"Hey, if you guys beat Nicolet on Monday then you'll be in second place all by yourselves in the eighth grade league, right?"

Dina nodded, but then grew quiet.

"Oh, shoot." Christine grimaced. "I'm sorry. They're so stupid, scheduling a game on Yom Kippur."

"No kidding. I may go to the game anyway." Dina set her jaw in defiance.

Christine's eyes grew wide. "What are you talking about? You can't—"

"Yes, I can. Why not? I had my Bat Mitzvah already, so I'm responsible for finding my own way to reach G-d."

Christine narrowed her eyes and nodded tight-lipped as if she were thinking it over.

A groan went up in the crowd as Michigan State blocked a

Kristen Arthurs hit. Dina groaned with them, but for a different reason. "I still haven't told Coach Vaughn about Yom Kippur on Monday."

"So don't tell her."

"What d'ya mean?"

"Don't tell her anything. If Coach Vaughn doesn't know you're skipping Temple, then she won't know you're not supposed to be at the game."

Dina liked the idea. "I just *have* to go to the game. Grace is out for at least two weeks. She sprained her wrist pretty bad, and if I don't show up for Monday's game, they won't have a decent middle blocker."

"But—" Christine frowned.

"What?"

"Your parents. They won't let you skip Temple."

"That's the hard part. My parents." Dina looked away. She didn't want to think about Yom Kippur anymore. It was only Friday, and she had until Monday morning to figure something out.

Mrs. Hannigan came back with Joey and handed them each a bottled water. They settled down to watch Michigan State rally back to beat Purdue in the third set by a score of 19-25.

Christine shook her head as the fourth set began and crossed all her fingers again.

Dina crossed all her fingers, too. "The whole set this time."

Christine nodded once. "We have to."

Michigan State took the lead in the fourth set right away, but Purdue tied it up. Michigan State took the lead again, and Purdue tied it up once again. This happened several more times, until Purdue finally took the lead for an extended stretch. Michigan State was not to be outdone and re-tied the game to make the score 19-19. On the next play, Kristen Arthurs saved the day with a sizzling kill over the net to put Purdue ahead by one. Dina cheered with the rest of the Purdue crowd, all her fingers still crossed.

"That's you," Christine shouted over the roaring crowd. "The middle hitter who scores points."

"I wish." Dina hoped that someday she'd be as good as Kristen Arthurs and play for Purdue. "Look, there you are." She pointed to Purdue's libero, Blair Bashen.

Christine grinned. "Let's both play for Purdue, okay?"

"Deal."

They bumped fists as well as they could with all their fingers crossed.

Dina decided that if she was ever going to make the Purdue volleyball team, she had to get as much experience as she could. And that included playing in Monday's game against Nicolet.

She sat back in her seat satisfied with her decision and watched the unranked Purdue volleyball team beat nationally ranked Michigan State in the fourth and final set.

Chapter 25
G-d Knows We Have Lives

Dina raced into her bedroom after Temple to get changed for practice. She didn't want to be late. Coach Vaughn moved the eighth grade team practice to the afternoon, so it wouldn't conflict with Dina's family going to Temple.

Dina wanted to throw her clothes on the floor, so she could get into her shorts and practice shirt faster, but instead she made herself slow down and carefully place her dress in the laundry hamper. She needed to be extra careful about not annoying her parents, since she was going to defy them by going to school on Monday.

She threw her practice bag onto her bed and whipped it open. Court shoes, hair bands, knee pads. Everything was there. She zipped it back up and threw on her Earhart Middle School sweatshirt, darted out of her bedroom, and ran into the kitchen.

"*Chamudi*," her father chastised, "you're barreling through the house like a bull. What's the hurry?" He plucked a piece of toast out of the toaster and started to butter it.

"I have to go to practice."

"On *Shabbat*?"

Dina hoped her father wouldn't make her stay home. She thought he knew about the practice that afternoon. Luckily, her mother walked into the kitchen at just that moment.

"Honey, G-d knows we have lives. I'm sure He understands about volleyball practices on Saturday."

Her father shrugged. "I guess." He held out his arms toward Dina. "Hug your old dad before you go."

"You're not old." Dina hugged her father. "I'll only be gone a couple of hours." She headed toward the door to the garage near the laundry room.

"Love you, *Chamudi*." He sat down at the kitchen table, picked up the *Indianapolis Star*, and turned to the sports pages.

Her mother pulled her sweater from a hook near the door and grabbed her purse. "I'll be back in a bit, honey."

"All right." He didn't look up. He was already immersed in the sports section. "Have a good practice," he called to Dina.

"Thanks, Dad."

As her mother backed the car out of the driveway, Dina thought maybe it was a good time to talk to her about skipping Yom Kippur. Dr. Lewiski, the athletic director, said that athletes had to go to school in order to play in a game that same day. There was no way around it. She had to go to school on Monday.

She went for it. "Mom?"

"Yes, honey?"

Dina's heart pounded in her chest. What if her mother blew a gasket? What if her mother turned the car around and didn't even let her go to the practice? What if she yanked her off the team?

"Never mind." She looked out the passenger window at the fallow soybean fields whizzing by.

"What is it, honey? It's just us girls here."

Dina rolled her eyes. Her mother thought she wanted to talk about boys or something. Boys were the furthest thing from her mind at the moment. She frantically searched her mind for something. "I just wanted to know if I could go with Christine to the Purdue game tomorrow night."

"You know that's not a good idea. It's Erev Yom Kippur."

"The eve of the day of atonement. Okay. Just thought I'd ask."

Her mother looked at her thoughtfully. "You're going to fast this year, aren't you?"

Dina nodded, but looked away. "Yeah," she lied. She had to eat if she was going to play volleyball. She took a deep breath and let it out slowly, hoping her mother hadn't heard the falseness in her words.

"That's my girl."

Her mother pulled the car up to the Earhart Middle School gymnasium. Dina gave her mother a quick hug goodbye. "Coach said two hours, so I guess you can pick me up at three."

"Okay, honey," her mother said. "Love you."

"Love you, too, Mom." Dina grabbed her bag and bolted out of the car.

She walked slowly to the gym so she could compose herself. Lying sucked, but she was doing it for all the right reasons. Coach Vaughn and Miki and Stephanie and everybody else on the eighth grade team were counting on her to play middle blocker in the game against Nicolet on Monday. They needed to win so they could be in second place all by themselves. She couldn't let them down, especially not with Grace hurt. She couldn't bail on them after only playing one game.

She walked into the gym, and a few of her new teammates were sitting on the bleachers getting ready for the practice.

"Hey, Stretch," Miki called from the bleachers. "What's up?"

"Nothing new. How are you guys?" Dina sat on the bottom bleacher and threw on her knee pads and court shoes. She pulled her hair back into a pony tail and tacked it high on her head.

"Bummer about Grace," Stephanie said to Miki. "Out for the next two weeks."

"Yeah, but the Lord answered my prayers and gave us Stretch," Miki answered with an evil grin.

"Whoo hoo," her teammates hooted in agreement.

Zola patted Dina on the back. "Nicolet's not going to know what hit them when we attack with our triple threat—Stephanie, Bernadette, and Stretch."

Miki nodded. "When we win Monday, we'll only be one game behind Star City."

"Yeah," Stephanie said, "and then we'll beat the tar out of them in the Lafayette League Tournament. They're not gonna know what hit 'em."

The eighth graders bumped fists with Dina, and she cringed inside. She just had to find a way to go to school on Monday.

Coach Vaughn walked into the gym. "Miki, get the team stretched and then take your usual laps."

"Okay, Coach." Miki stood up. "Let's go, women."

Dina welcomed the physical activity. It gave her a chance to shake off her worries for a moment. Once their laps were done, Coach Vaughn set up a hitting drill, but this time she put Dina on the far side of the net to practice blocking hits all by herself.

Dina slid back and forth as Miki set the ball to either Stephanie or Bernadette. She tried to figure out if Miki's sets were going left or right, high or short. She guessed right most of the time, but was fooled every now and then.

"A few more, Dina, and then you and Stephanie'll trade places."

"Okay." Dina stood with her hands on her hips, catching her breath.

Coach Vaughn tossed the ball to the back row. Zola passed the ball to Miki. Miki got under it, and Dina knew by the way Miki was leaning that she was setting up Stephanie. Dina slid to the right. Short set. Shoot. She leaped quickly, but didn't get much height. She barely got a piece of the ball. Miki's short sets were so sneaky.

"Dina," Coach Vaughn said, "you've got to slide over there more quickly. Both Nicolet and Star City hit with a lot of power and have a lot of options. Stay alert."

"Okay, Coach." Dina blew out a breath. Playing with the older girls was definitely a lot harder.

"Let's switch it up." Coach Vaughn directed the girls to their new positions, with Stephanie on the other side as the lone blocker.

"Bring it on, Stretch," Stephanie teased.

Miki sent Dina a nice high set up the middle. Stephanie set up right in front of her. Dina ripped a cannon shot over her block. It smashed to the floor.

Stephanie flicked her blonde pony tail behind her in annoyance and scowled at Dina. "Try that again." She glared at her without smiling. "I dare you."

Dina stared at her wide-eyed. Stephanie laughed, and Dina blew out a sigh of relief.

The two-hour practice went by in a flash. Dina was tired, but it was a good tired. She wasn't ready to go home, though, because the weight of the world sat squarely on her shoulders. Somehow she had to find a way to talk her parents into letting her go to the game on Monday. Luckily, she didn't have to say anything to Coach Vaughn. That was one conflict avoided.

Dina put her knee pads and court shoes in her bag. She was still sweating, so she decided to sit on the bleachers and cool off before putting on her sweatshirt.

Coach Vaughn locked up the bin of volleyballs. "Nice practice, Dina. You're really rising to the occasion."

"Thanks, Coach."

"Are you getting along with the other girls all right?" Most of her new teammates had filtered out of the gym by that time.

Dina nodded. "Yeah. Everybody's been seriously nice to me."

"So, I guess we'll see you at practice on Tuesday then? You haven't said anything, but I assume you're staying home for Yum Kipper on Monday, right?"

Stunned, all Dina could say was, "Right."

"I'd say enjoy your holiday, but this isn't one of those fun ones, is it?"

Dina shook her head. "No, we have to fast for twenty-four hours."

"Youch. That sounds tough." Coach Vaughn turned and headed toward the equipment closet. "Well, good luck. See you Tuesday."

"Okay, see ya." A chill ran through Dina. What was she supposed to do now? Her parents and her coach wanted her to stay home, but her teammates didn't know that and were expecting her in the starting lineup.

Coach Vaughn turned the lights out in the big gym and headed into her office.

Dina slapped the bottom bleacher. Why did life have to suck so much? Her mother was probably outside waiting for her, but she needed a minute to regroup. Christine told her not to tell Coach Vaughn about Yom Kippur, but somehow Coach Vaughn knew. Why was everybody making decisions for her? She smacked the bleacher again. She had her Bat Mitzvah in the spring. Wasn't she supposed to be responsible for her own decisions? G-d knew she had a life, and living her life meant playing volleyball on Monday.

She groaned. She was so confused. Not knowing what else to do, she pulled out her cell phone and said, "Christine," into the voice dial. Her spirits plummeted even further when she realized that not too long ago, she would have said, "*Schmeggegy*" into the phone to call Robyn for advice.

Chapter 26
G-d Will Understand

Dina put the lid on the pot of rice and moved it off the burner. "The rice is done, Mom."

Her mother turned the oven to its lowest setting. "The chicken and stewed tomatoes are done, too. Now all we have to do is wait for your father to get back from the store with the lox for tomorrow's bagels, and we can have our pre-fast meal." She wiped her hands on a dish rag.

"The table's all set, too." Dina pointed at the dining room table set up with their best dishes and tall candles. It would be her job to light the candles and say the blessing before sunset.

"Our first Yom Kippur dinner in our new house," her mother said wistfully. "It'll finally feel like home."

Dina returned her mother's smile, but then felt guilty about her plans to defy everyone and go to school on Monday. She looked down as if the floor were suddenly very interesting. "Mom, can I call Robyn? You know, to tell her, *Gmar hatima tova*?"

"You'd better hurry. The sun sets a little sooner in New York."

"It does?"

Her mother nodded. "They might be eating or even off to Temple by now."

"Shoot. I'll be back in a few minutes." She bolted toward her room.

"Water bottle," her mother called after her.

Dina scurried back and grabbed the water bottle off the kitchen counter. "I forgot." Her mother said the hardest part about fasting was not being able to drink anything, so she told Dina to drink a lot of water beforehand. She ran from the kitchen into her bedroom, shut the door behind her, and grabbed her cell phone from the bedside stand. Christine hadn't been much help the day before. She had even gone as far as to suggest the unthinkable. She suggested that Dina simply stay home for Yom Kippur.

Dina was still confused, so she decided to call Robyn. Robyn would know what to do. "*Schmeggegy,*" she said into the phone.

"Dina!" Robyn answered on the first ring. "What's up, dork?"

It was good to hear Robyn's voice after so long. "*Gmar hatima tova.*"

"Oh, thanks. Have an easy fast yuhself. I dunno if I'm gonna make it the whole freakin' time, ya know?"

Dina stifled a giggle. Robyn's New York accent was so thick. She wondered if that's how she sounded when she first got to Indiana. "I don't know if I'm going to last, either." She did her best to enunciate clearly like her mother wanted her to. "I might not even fast on—"

"Hey, Dina," Robyn interrupted. "Listen, can I call you back, like, after?"

"Oh, okay." Dina felt like the wind had gotten knocked out of her sails. She desperately wanted to talk to Robyn about her volleyball game conflict during Yom Kippur.

"Megan's comin' ovuh for Erev Yom Kippur dinnuh tuhnight, and I still gotta get ready. *Capisce?*"

Megan? The girl that Robyn had made fun of because she was a cheerleader, dyed her hair, and wore too much makeup? That Megan? "Okay."

"Thanks, boss. Gotta go. *Gmar hatima tova.*"

"Thanks." Before Dina could say goodbye, she heard the clear sound of Robyn disconnecting the call. She closed her phone and threw it on the bed. "Whatevuh," she said sarcastically at the phone. "I mean, whateverrrr," she corrected. If she hadn't been so miserable about Robyn never having time for her anymore, she might have chuckled over her slip into New Yorkese. She took a sip from her water bottle.

Her mother tapped on her bedroom door.

"C'mon in, Mom."

"How's Robyn?"

"She's okay. She's getting ready for dinner."

"Is she going to fast this year?"

Dina nodded. "She said she was."

"Are you all set for your fast?"

Dina nodded and held up her water bottle. "I'm almost done." She took another sip, and then looked down at her comforter. She avoided her mother's gaze. She smoothed out the green cotton material with the palm of her hand.

Her mother walked over to the bed and sat down. "What's up, honey?"

"Nothing."

Her mother waited.

After a few painful moments, Dina finally said, "Robyn."

"What's going on?"

"She doesn't like me anymore."

"What are you talking about? Of course she likes you."

"She never wants to talk on the phone." Dina continued to smooth out the already smoothed comforter.

"Well, it *is* Erev Yom Kippur," her mother said. "She and her family are probably busy getting ready."

"Yeah." Another long silence grew between them. Dina pulled her knees up to her chest and hugged them.

"Anything else on your mind?"

"No," Dina said way too quickly. She cringed because she knew her mother would press her until she spilled it.

"Hmm, let's see. I've been your mother for, how long? Almost twelve-and-a-half years? I think by now I know when something's bothering you."

Dina took a deep breath for courage. "I want to play in the volleyball game tomorrow." She held her breath.

"What?" Her mother look puzzled. After a long pause she said way too calmly, "You can't, honey."

"Why not?"

"Adina Ann Jacobs, you know that's not possible." Her mother's voice had a stern edge. "Yom Kippur is the holiest of holy days. We'll be in Temple most of the day."

Dina picked at the comforter, not knowing what to say.

"Adina, what's the meaning of Yom Kippur?"

"To show repentance to G-d. To ask him for forgiveness." Dina kept her eyes on the bedspread.

"How do you think G-d is going to feel if you tell him that volleyball is more important to you than He is?"

Dina didn't know how to tell her mother that she had to play in every game she could, so she could get as good as Logan Tom and Kristen Arthurs and Carrie Gurnell. How could she tell her mother that she was in training so she could play volleyball at Purdue and then get picked for the Olympic team?

Before she could formulate a response, her mother stood up. "I think you need to sit in this room and think about your relationship with G-d. I'll call you for dinner when Daddy gets home."

Dina felt tears forming. She stayed focused on the bedspread and didn't respond.

"Look at me, young lady."

Dina wiped at her eyes with her sleeve and looked up. Her mother's face was a mixture of disappointment and anger. "Not a word of this foolishness to your father."

Dina groaned.

"Do you hear me?"

"Yes. Yes. Okay. Fine."

Her mother turned on her heels, walked through the doorway, and shut the door firmly behind her. Dina fell back against her pillows with a groan.

Her phone chimed, announcing an incoming text. She looked at the closed door. Her parents said she wasn't supposed to use her phone during Yom Kippur, but it wasn't officially Yom Kippur yet, so it wouldn't hurt to at least see who the text was from. Maybe Robyn snuck in a quick text to apologize for hanging up so fast.

Dina opened the phone. The text was from Christine, but there was more than one from her. Dina scrolled back to the first text, which had come in at twelve-thirty. "Going 2 Michigan-Purdue game now. I'll tell Kristen Arthurs u said hi! LOL." Dina smiled. The next text read, "Michigan ranked #8. Go Purdue!" The next few texts were shorter. "Purdue won the 1st set!" then, "P lost 2nd set." Followed by, "P won 3rd," then "P lost 4th."

Dina thought she heard a noise outside of her room and put the phone down in a hurry. She listened intently, then picked the phone back up when all seemed quiet. With Purdue tied two sets to two against a ranked team like Michigan, she just had to find out what had happened next. Would Purdue be able win the last set? She flipped open her phone to read the text that had just come in. It was a long one.

"Hey Dina. Purdue VB went on a European Tour in May to Austria, Slovenia, Czech Repub, Italy. Let's play 4 Purdue and go 2 Europe, OK?"

"Okay," Dina said out loud. She could seriously get a jump start on her coin collecting that way, not to mention the international volleyball experience she'd get. That's exactly what she'd need to make the Olympic team.

Dina held the phone in a death grip. She just had to make the Purdue team. She'd already missed one game because of Rosh Hashanah. She couldn't miss another one. It wasn't her fault they scheduled stupid volleyball games during high holy days. G-d would understand, wouldn't He?

Chapter 27
When Worlds Collide

Dina laid out her white dress and headed to her closet to look for her dressy white sweater while her mother supervised. She stopped when she heard the outside garage door roll up. A minute later the door into the house squeaked opened.

"Daddy's home." Dina ran to the kitchen to greet him. Anything to get away from her mother.

"I found the last hidden stash of lox in all of Indiana," her father announced.

"You finally found some?"

He hung his coat on the hook by the door and gave her a big hug. "I did, indeed. Now I can relax, knowing we will have bagels and lox to break our fast."

"Mom made noodle kugel, too."

"Fantastic. We're all set now." His face turned serious. "We must remember the real reason for Yom Kippur, though. This is your first fast, and I want you to fully understand why you're doing it."

Dina took a deep breath and nodded. "I think I get the whole asking G-d to forgive me for my sins against him thing." Even though she had resigned herself to fasting and spending the day at Temple, she still needed to ask G-d's forgiveness for her divided heart. She still desperately wanted to play in the game.

Her father smiled. She loved the little crinkles that formed around his eyes. "That's my *Chamudi*." He gave her a quick hug.

Her mother came out from the hallway that led to Dina's room, and Dina turned away. She just couldn't look her mother in the eye. She used a potholder to bring the bowl of rice to the table for their pre-fast meal. Her mother helped her place the rest of the food on the table, and then her parents sat down.

Dina lit the candles and then said the blessing, thanking G-d for providing food. She and her mother acted as if nothing was wrong. She ate heartily, probably too heartily, but she was nervous about her first fasting.

After dinner, they headed to the synagogue for the *Kol Nidre* evening service. Finding a place to park proved to be trickier than usual. They finally found a spot in the far corner of the lot.

Dina closed the back door of the car and fell in step behind her parents. "Hey, Dad, who are all these people? The twice-a-year J—"

"Dina," her mother snapped. "Manners, please." She shot Dina a disapproving look, making Dina's toes curl inside her already uncomfortable shoes.

"Sorry, Mom."

Her father looked at her with a twinkle in his eye and nodded once in answer to her question.

Dina clamped her lips together, so she wouldn't laugh. She caught the glare her mother sent and stopped smiling.

Right from the first prayer, Dina knew two things. She wasn't going to eat or drink anything until after sundown on Monday and, more importantly, she had to find a way to make missing the volleyball game less important than her time with G-d. Especially when her new teammates were going to hate her. The car ride home from the synagogue after the somber service was quiet until her father spoke.

"How are you doing on your fast so far, *Chamudi*?" He grinned at her.

"Ha-ha. I'm still stuffed from dinner. Ask me tomorrow morning after we *don't* eat breakfast."

"Okay, I will." He pulled the car up the driveway and into the garage.

Dina went straight to her room as soon as they got home. She flung herself on her bed and prayed for G-d to settle her conflicted heart. She hoped the eighth grade team would win without her. That way her teammates wouldn't have a reason to hate her. She prayed with all her might for an Earhart victory over Nicolet on Monday.

She heard footsteps coming down the hall and recognized them as her mother's. She rolled on her side, away from the door, so she wouldn't have to look at her mother.

Her mother knocked lightly. "May I come in?"

"Sure." Dina didn't roll back.

Her mother came in and sat on the far side of bed. "Honey, did you listen to the service today?"

Dina nodded.

"And did you hear the message? Asking G-d for forgiveness?"

Again, Dina nodded, but kept her eyes focused on her closet door.

"I know you really want to play in the game tomorrow, honey." Her mother sighed.

Dina sat up. "We didn't have games on Yom Kippur back home. We didn't even have school."

"Yes, well, back home there's a much larger Jewish population."

Dina took in her mother's tight-lipped smile. The smile didn't quite reach her eyes.

"Mom, I'm sorry, but I really want to go to school tomorrow. I want to play in the game. Nobody else is staying home. I *have* to play."

"Okay, I'll bite. Why do you *have* to play?"

Her mother looked wound up tight like a spring ready to pop, but Dina forged ahead. "I have to play because Nicolet's really good, and we're tied with them, and Grace is hurt, and they have nobody else to play middle blocker, and I want to get good enough to play for the Landsharks club team with Christine and then make the high school team in ninth grade and play for Purdue so we can get back at Michigan for beating them in five sets yesterday and then play in the Olympics with Logan Tom in 2020." The words came tumbling out before she could stop them. She hadn't admitted any of her plans to anybody except Christine. She held her breath, waiting for her mother's response.

Her mother let out one of her patented I'm-disappointed-in-you sighs, and Dina knew she was toast. Her mother stood up. "C'mon, let's go talk this out with your father." She opened the door to the hallway and beckoned Dina toward it.

Dina's heart clenched. She had already disappointed her mother, she couldn't disappoint her father, too. She didn't move. "Mom, don't get Daddy involved. Please? I'll just stay home and fast. I will. I promise."

Her mother stood silently by the door and folded her arms across her chest. They were at a standstill.

"Why is our world colliding with theirs?" Dina asked, breaking the silence first. "It's so not fair."

"Oh, honey. Life's not always fair." Her mother sat back down on the bed and pulled Dina into a quick hug. "I know volleyball means a lot to you. Maybe we can figure something out, like asking Coach Vaughn to stay a few minutes after practices to help you work on your skills or something. Maybe that way you can improve and do all those great things you've planned for yourself."

"You don't think it's crazy to want to play in the Olympics?"

"Not at all. I'm just concerned that your plans are interfering with your relationship with G-d."

"I know."

Her mother didn't respond.

They sat in silence until Dina couldn't take it any more.

"Christine and I want to play for Team USA in 2020," she blurted.

"That's an admirable goal." Her mother smiled. "About tomorrow, though, I want you to think about it this way. What if you and Daddy planned a special day to be together, a day you'd planned for all year long, and now that it's finally here, you tell him at the last minute you want to play volleyball instead?"

Dina's heart clenched. It would break her father's heart if

she did that. She would hate disappointing him that way. She looked down at her hands for a moment. "That would kind of stink, I guess."

Her mother patted her folded hands and stood up. "I may be crazy, but I've decided to let you make your own decision about going to school tomorrow."

"You did?" Dina couldn't believe what she hearing. "But what about Daddy?"

"I'll handle your father. All I ask is that you take time tonight to weigh all of your options, including the fact that tomorrow is supposed to be your special day with G-d."

"Okay."

"I'll wake you up early enough if you do want to go to school. You can let us know then what you've decided. Okay?"

Dina nodded. "Okay, Mom. Thank you. Good night."

Her mother gave her another quick hug and closed the door softly behind her as she left.

Dina had an almost impossible choice ahead of her. Whatever she chose to do, she would disappoint someone.

Chapter 28
Respect

Coach Vaughn tapped her clipboard and pointed at the visiting team. "They shouldn't have taken that second set from you. We're only two points away from winning the third and final set, so get out there and show them who the better team is." The official blew the whistle, ending the time-out. "And no more service errors." She stepped out of the team time-out circle.

Miki put her hand on top of Dina's in the circle. "Flyers on three. One, two, three."

"Flyers," Dina yelled with her teammates and then hustled back onto the floor.

Why did Coach Vaughn have to mention service errors when it was her turn to serve? The line judge gave Dina the ball.

Dina took a deep breath. Someday she would learn how to jump serve, but for now all she had was her floater. Kristen Arthurs from Purdue used a floater serve, so it couldn't be all that bad.

Dina waited for the up official's whistle and threw the ball in the air. She smacked the ball with her cupped hand. She cringed when the ball hit the tape on the top of the net. A kind bounce caused it to flip over to the visitor's side of the court and hit the floor. Point Flyers. One more point, and they would win the set and the match.

"Go, *Chamudi*," her father yelled from the sidelines.

Dina wanted to turn and smile at him and at her mother, but she forced herself to remain focused. Miki flashed the sign for the next play. Dina's heart leaped to her throat. Miki called for a back row hit from her. She tried to quiet the butterflies in her stomach, but was having a hard time. The official blew the whistle for the serve. It sailed smoothly over the net to the visiting team's back row.

The libero passed the ball to her setter. The setter hit it off line, causing their outside hitter to pass the ball over the net for a free ball. Stephanie got under it and passed it to Miki. Dina took her steps, and, as planned, Miki set the ball up for a back row hit.

Dina leaped high, swung her arm with all her might, and snapped her wrist. The ball rocketed over the net. The visiting team's libero scrambled to get under it. The ball ricocheted off her forearms and out of bounds. Point and match for the Flyers. Dina punched a fist in the air while the Flyers's home town crowd cheered the win.

Stephanie pulled Dina into a quick hug. "Way to go, Stretch. Thank the Lord we got you back."

Miki patted Dina on the back, and they headed to the end line for the official end-of-game line up. "Great job, Stretch. I know Coach Blanchard will take you now."

Dina was confused. "Who's Coach Blanchard?" They headed to the net for the ritual low fives with the opposing team. As she smacked each girl's hand, she said, "Good game," but didn't hear her own words. She was trying to figure out who Miki was talking about. She didn't have time to ask, because Coach Vaughn called them together.

The Flyers team huddled around their coach. "Okay, girls, great win today. I'm proud of you for not folding after we lost that second set. You played smart and used your strengths."

Miki laughed. "That's 'cuz we got Dina back." The other players patted Dina on the back.

"Yeah, Dina." Stephanie looked at her. "We couldn't do anything right against Nicolet when you were gone for your Yom Kippur thingy. You should have seen us. We played like the sixth grade team."

"But after Monday's loss to Nicolet," Coach Vaughn interrupted, "you all regrouped and beat St. Mary's handedly on Wednesday and Murdock Heights today."

Miki bumped Dina playfully. "That's 'cuz we got Stretch back."

Dina smiled at Miki. As it turned out, her teammates weren't mad at her at all for missing the Nicolet game, and she'd made it right with G-d by staying home on His special day, even though the whole not-eating thing was kind of hard.

"We're solidly in third place now," Coach Vaughn continued. A few of the girls groaned. Third place hadn't been the team goal that season. "So that means we'll meet Nicolet in the first round of the playoffs this Saturday."

"Saturday?" Miki glanced at Dina with a worried expression.

"Don't worry. My family and I can probably go to Temple on Friday night."

Miki let out such an exaggerated sigh of relief that the entire team, including Coach Vaughn, laughed.

Right at that moment, Dina was glad of two things—her teammates and coach seemed to understand her commitment to her religion, and she would finally get the chance to play against the Nicolet team. Maybe she could help her team beat them this time.

Dina still felt a little bad not going to the game on Yom Kippur, but after her mother had told her the choice was hers, she remembered something Mr. Robertson had said on the very first day of school. He'd told them to always be respectful, even if they didn't like something. Dina didn't like the fact that she had to disappoint her coach and teammates, but her respect for G-d and for her parents were so much more important in the grand scheme of things. The relief on her parents' faces Monday morning when she told them she was going to stay home had been priceless. The relief she felt at making the right decision was even more rewarding.

Coach Vaughn flipped to another page on her clipboard. "Let's focus our energy on Saturday's playoff games. If we beat Nicolet in the first game, we'll probably face Star City in the finals. They're undefeated. Again. And unfortunately the tournament is in their home gym with their very loud fans."

Stephanie shook her head. "Those Star City girls eat, breathe, and sleep volleyball."

"Yeah, I think they do." Coach Vaughn nodded. "We have four practices until then. Be ready to work hard."

Dina groaned along with her teammates. Coach Vaughn was a fun coach, but she seriously pushed them to their limits, trying to make them better.

"Okay, girls. Your parents are waiting." Coach Vaughn stepped out of the circle and went to shake hands with two women who had been hovering near their team bench.

"Flyers on three," Miki said. "One, two, three."

"Flyers!" Dina yelled with her teammates. The team broke up its close circle and headed to the bench. She tugged at Miki's uniform sleeve. "Hey, who's Coach Blanchard you mentioned before?"

Miki pointed to one of the tall women talking with Coach Vaughn. "Coach Blanchard is the one with the gray hair, and she's only the coach of the West Lafayette Landsharks, the primo club volleyball team around here."

Oh. Dina knew who the West Lafayette Landsharks were. That was the club team Christine had been telling her about ever since they'd met. "Do you play for them?"

Miki nodded. "Yep, and so does Stephanie. We need you, though, big time. And we need a good libero. Zola's parents won't let her play with us. They think volleyball distracts her from her school work."

"I know a good libero."

Miki grinned. "So do I. We already told Coach Blanchard about Christine."

"You did?"

Miki nodded. "Christine's really good."

Dina smiled at the praise for her friend. "Hey, I heard you guys went to a tournament in Chicago last year."

Miki pulled a sweatshirt out of her bag and tugged it over her head. "Yep, we came in third out of fifteen teams."

"That's good."

"When you play with us, we'll come in first," Miki said matter-of-factly.

"I don't know about that." Dina wanted to play for the Landsharks, but now that someone else had actually suggested it, she had big doubts about whether or not she was good enough.

Chapter 29
Silence

Dina pulled her sweatshirt on even though the Star City gymnasium seemed warm enough. Coach Vaughn wanted them to stay loose after beating Nicolet in the first match. She only had a few minutes before the championship game against Star City, so she hustled to the bleachers to see her parents, Christine, Brittany, and Marguerite.

"Great job, *Chamudi*." Her father grabbed her in a hug. "Blah, you're all sweaty."

"No kidding." She bugged her eyes out at him. "You just watched us beat Nicolet, didn't you?"

His fake grimace told her he was teasing, and he hugged her again. "My all-star."

Dina hugged her mother.

"You played so well, honey."

"Thanks, Mom."

"Omigosh," Christine gushed. "You looked like Kristen Arthurs at middle. I couldn't believe it when you tooled the block in that last play. That was crazy."

"Yeah," Marguerite said, "you're so awesome."

"Thanks guys. I can't believe it only took us two sets to beat Nicolet."

"Phht," Brittany said. "That's 'cuz you played this time."

"But now we have to play undefeated Star City." Dina made a sour face.

"Maybe it's time for them to get their first lost." Christine shrugged. "I'm just sayin'."

"Yeah." Dina bumped fists with her friends. She leaned in closer. "Hey, you guys, there she is." She pointed to a gray-haired woman sitting on the Star City side of the bleachers.

"Who?"

"Coach Blanchard. The West Lafayette Landsharks coach I was telling you about."

Christine grimaced. "She's here? Why didn't you tell us?"

"I didn't see her until just now."

"Tryouts are on Tuesday for you, right?" Marguerite bounced her knees up and down nervously as if she were the one trying out instead of Dina.

"Yeah," Christine said. "I wish we could try out, too."

"Criminy, Christine," Brittany said. "You can only try out by invitation. They usually only take eighth and ninth graders, anyway."

"Dina's going to make it," Christine said with assuredness, as if daring Brittany or anyone else to defy her.

Dina's mother leaned in. "And hopefully all of you girls will be invited to try out next year, right?"

They all nodded.

"I hope so." Christine crossed her fingers.

"Dina," her mother continued, "you'd better get back. Coach Vaughn just called for the Flyers to go back to the court."

"Oops." Dina leaped to her feet. "Gotta go, you guys. Wish me luck." She headed down the bleachers to the court.

"Good luck," Christine called after her.

"Thanks," Dina called back. She squeezed into the circle her teammates had formed in front of the visitors' side of the court.

"We've all heard the stories about this team," Coach Vaughn said. "Like the one that claims Star City is the best middle school volleyball team in the state. We know they're undefeated, and we know they're used to winning, but this next match will prove to everyone who the best team is."

Dina hooted along with her teammates.

"They have a whole lot of swagger," Coach Vaughn continued, "but truthfully, I think they're bigger in their own minds. They're putting on a show for their fans." She looked up at the Star City fans in the bleachers. "Look. Their side of the bleachers is packed. Their fans are positively buzzing with excitement because they think they have the championship in the bag."

Dina frowned. The gym was covered with posters that said things like, "Lafayette League Champs—Star City" and "Star City—First Place Again" and "Star City Dominates."

"What these people forgot, though," Coach Vaughn said, "is that their Star City team has to go through you first. Remember this," she pointed at the Star City team huddle, "they're eighth graders just like you are. They have classes all day long, eat lunch in a cafeteria, and do homework, just like you. This team is very beatable, but we have to play our absolute best game to do it. No mistakes. This home town crowd is used to seeing their team win. Let's change that today. Your goal is to silence this crowd." She paused as if letting it sink in. "All right, girls. Let's go get 'em. Let's show them they have some competition today." She stepped outside the circle.

Miki put one hand in the middle, and the girls put their hands on top. "Let's change it up today, Flyers. Let's shout 'silence' on three instead of Flyers. Okay?"

Dina thought it was kind of weird to shout the word *silence*, but they did, and a few of the Star City fans laughed at them. She did her best to ignore them and ran to the end line with the rest of the starters. Maybe they could scare the undefeated Star City powerhouse by winning the first set. Maybe they actually could silence the crowd once and for all.

Dina's heart pounded as the first server for Star City stepped behind the end line. The Star City fans stood up. Dina groaned. She remembered Coach Vaughn telling them that the fans stood up until their team scored its first point. She hoped her team could keep the Star City fans on their feet for a long, long time. Maybe that would silence them.

The official blew the whistle to start the game. The Star City server tossed the ball high in the air, ran two steps, and leaped. Her strong arm sent the jump serve rocketing to the back row. The ball careened off Zola's bicep and smashed into the wall behind her. Point Star City. The packed gymnasium of Star

City fans roared their approval and sat down with a collective thump.

"Hmm," Dina mumbled under her breath. "So much for quieting the crowd." She got ready for the next serve.

The next jump serve screamed over the net. Zola got under it. Barely. The ball glanced off her arms in Miki's direction. Miki set the ball up to Stephanie, but off line. Stephanie tried to adjust, but couldn't, and pushed the ball over the net. Star City turned the free ball into a point and took the lead by a score of 0-2.

On the third serve, Miki set the ball up to Dina in the middle. Dina's adrenaline seemed to be working overtime. She mistimed her steps and hit the ball weakly into the Star City block. The ball fell on the Flyers side of the court giving Star City their third unanswered point.

Coach Vaughn stood up. "Time out."

The up official blew her whistle and indicated a time-out charged to the Flyers.

Dina cringed. If Coach was calling a time-out after only three points, she must be seriously annoyed.

"Girls," Coach Vaughn said, "we're acting like the game has already been played, and we've lost. Get aggressive. I'd rather see you go for the kills and miss than play it safe and give them a free ball. They have a lot of big bodies at the net, so find ways around them." She turned toward Miki. "Use a few short sets. Stephanie, Bernadette, Dina, that'll mean quick hits from you."

Dina nodded, along with Stephanie and Bernadette.

After the time-out, the Star City player served a rocket down the line, and none of the Flyer players could handle it. The score was 0-4 in Star City's favor.

After the next Star City serve, Miki short set to Dina who leaped, saw an open spot, and ripped the ball down the middle of the court. Point Flyers.

"Finally," Miki said. "Side out."

Mary, one of the Flyers defensive specialists, served a floater over the net.

Star City's libero passed the ball to their setter. Dina saw the outside hitter approach the net, so she slid to her right in anticipation of the block. Her heart leaped into her throat when the setter back set the ball in the other direction toward the opposite hitter. Dina tried to shuffle to the other side, but the Star City player hit an uncontested cannon shot for another Star City point. She smacked herself on the thigh. She had set up the block in the wrong place.

"Time out," Coach Vaughn called from the sidelines. The team scurried over and formed a loose circle around her. "Girls, their setter is very deceptive. Her back sets especially. Find a way to figure out which way she's going with it. She has to be doing something to give it away."

The official blew the whistle, ending the time-out.

"Okay, girls," Coach Vaughn said. "We can do this." She stepped out of the circle.

"Silence on three," Miki said. "But let's whisper it this time."

"Silence," the team whispered and hustled back to their positions.

"C'mon, Stretch," Stephanie said. "Let's do this."

Dina nodded and took a deep breath. She looked where Christine, Brittany, and Marguerite sat with her mom and dad. Christine shot her a thumbs up. Dina flashed a quick smile and turned her attention back toward the court. She focused hard on the Star City setter. She was determined to figure out when the setter was going to use the front set, the back set, and, more importantly, the short set. If she didn't figure out something quickly, the Flyers would lose by an embarrassing score, and Coach Blanchard wouldn't look at her twice.

Chapter 30
King of the Mountain

Dina watched like a student in class. At first she couldn't tell which way the Star City setter was going to set the ball. Sometimes she guessed correctly, and sometimes the girl fooled her. Trusting her gut, she started to guess correctly more often than not, and she finally saw a pattern. The setter stood just a little bit taller with her shoulders back when she was going for the back set.

Dina pulled Stephanie and Bernadette to her. "I think I've got her figured out."

"Really?" Stephanie said. "Hallelujah."

Dina told them what she had figured out, and they scurried back to their positions.

Star City had a commanding lead in the first set by a score of 1-9. A Star City player served the ball over the net. Zola passed the ball to Miki who set the ball to Stephanie. Stephanie went for the kill, but the Star City libero got under it and passed the ball to their setter. The setter pulled her shoulders back.

Dina slid to her right, yelling, "Bernadette."

Bernadette slid toward her. They leaped, Dina's stomach tingling like mad. The ball smacked into her outstretched hands and bounced back on the Star City side of the floor. Point and side out for the Flyers.

"Into the roof," Christine yelled from the stands. Dina didn't look at her, but smiled inside.

Star City's run in the first set came to a screeching halt with Dina's rally-killing discovery. The Flyers slowly grabbed momentum and scored point after painstaking point to catch up to the hometown favorites. The lead bounced back and forth until the score was tied up at 23-23. The Flyers had the serve.

Zola served the ball cleanly over the net. The Star City

libero passed the ball to her setter. Dina watched the setter's shoulders. She slid to her left and bumped hips with Stephanie, and they leaped. The Star City hitter must have seen them coming and panicked because she sent a free ball over the net. Miki got under it and set the ball up high for Dina in the middle. At the net, Dina pulled her arm back to hit the ball with all her might, but saw the Star City libero hanging way back. She made a split-second decision and dinked the ball into an open space the size of an Indiana corn field. The ball bounced on the floor and hit the libero in the chest. Dina pumped a fist. Point Flyers.

"Great read, Dina," Coach Vaughn called.

Dina blew out a sigh to try to calm her nerves. They were up by a score of 24-23. One more point, and the first set was theirs.

Zola served the ball again, and the Star City team sent a weak hit back over. Zola passed the ball to Miki who set up Dina nice and high in the middle. Dina saw an opening down the sideline and flew in like Logan Tom, Kristen Arthurs, and Carrie Gurnell all rolled into one. She released her arm like a spring. The ball smashed against the floor and flew into the stands. The line judge raised the flag. Dina groaned. The ball had landed out of bounds.

"That missed by inches, Dina." Miki patted her on the back.

"That's okay, Dina," Coach Vaughn called. "You had the opening, you just put a little too much mustard on it."

Dina didn't know how Coach Vaughn could remain so calm, because the score was tied at 24-24, and Star City had the side out.

The Star City server set up behind the end line. She tossed the ball in the air and sailed a floater serve high over the net.

"Long," Dina yelled to the back row, hoping they'd let it go out.

Zola swung her body out of the way at the last second, and the ball sailed out of bounds. Point Flyers.

"Nice let, Zola," Dina called. She tightened her fists and

shook them toward her teammate. They were up by a score of 25-24, but needed one more point to win by two.

"C'mon, Flyers," Coach Vaughn encouraged. "We're not going anywhere. Don't back down. Stay strong."

Dina heard her parents and friends yell encouragement.

"It's crunch time, Flyers," Coach Vaughn yelled. "Go for it. There's no turning back."

With the side out, the Flyers got the serve back. Bernadette served the ball over the net to the back row. The Star City libero passed it up to her front row with too much momentum. With no blockers in the way, Dina leaped and unloaded. It was easy cherry picking. The ball smashed onto the court for the final point of the set.

The official blew the whistle. The Flyers had just won the first set. Stephanie leaped in the air and hugged Dina. "We won! We *won*!"

Miki hugged Dina once Stephanie let go. "Nice read, Stretch." They headed toward their team bench.

The Star City team went back to their bench, looking positively stunned. They hadn't lost a single set all year long, and apparently didn't seem to know how to react. Their fans acted equally stunned.

Dina grabbed her water bottle and drank heartily. She gladly took a dry towel from Lori, their team manager. She wiped the sweat off her face and arms and draped the towel over her legs.

If the Flyers won the next set, they would be the Lafayette League Champion. A feat that, according to Coach Vaughn, hadn't happened for Earhart Middle School in the last ten years or more. Before the game, Miki and Stephanie had told Dina that Star City always won the championship, and all the other teams resigned themselves to playing for second place. *Not this year*, Dina thought. It was time for the Flyers to be the king of the mountain for a change.

Coach Vaughn squatted in front of the starters. The non-starters stood behind her. "Girls, I think you not only surprised this Star City team, but their fans as well." She chuckled. "Let's not forget, though, that they're a good team, and they'll find the chinks in our armor, just like you found theirs." She turned to Miki. "Miki, throw in a few more quicks, okay? We're giving them too much time to set up." She finished her speech by telling them to keep up their intensity.

The official blew her whistle, and the Flyers ran back onto the court for the start of the second set. The Star City team had opened the door a crack, and all the Flyers had to do was bust it all the way open.

Miki served the ball to start the second set. The Star City setter got underneath it and set a beauty for the tall Star City outside hitter. Dina slid to her right and leaped hip to hip with Stephanie. Unfortunately, the tall Star city player leaped even higher and smashed the ball to the floor. Dina cringed. Side out Star City. She hated when side outs didn't go her way.

The down official blew her whistle. Dina whipped her head around to see what the call was.

"Net," she said and indicated a point for the Flyers.

Apparently the Star City hitter's follow through forced her into the net. It wasn't a side out after all.

The Flyers got the early lead in the game, but didn't keep it for long. Star City scored a few more points to take the lead. The Flyers came back to tie it up and then go ahead. The lead seemed to change with every side out. Both teams were playing their fourth set of the day, and neither seemed tired or willing to give in.

Late in the game, the Star City team took the lead by a score of 23-24. They needed one more point to win the set and force a third. The Star City player served the ball. Zola passed it to Miki who back set to Bernadette. Bernadette snapped her wrist and found an open spot. Point Flyers. The score was tied 24-24.

Dina pumped her fist. "Side out. Way to go Bernadette."

"Just like that, women. Keep 'em coming," Miki said to her hitters.

Dina nodded and got ready for Miki's serve. The floater sailed over the net. It looked like the ball was going out of bounds. The

Star City libero popped it up in the air near the end line. Another back row player tried to pass the ball to the front row, but it skipped into the stands. The Flyers went ahead 25-24.

Stephanie clapped her hands. "One more point, Flyers. C'mon, we can do this."

Dina's stomach tingled. She was about to be part of a history-making game. Okay, it was only a middle school volleyball game, and wouldn't make the news or anything, but the game was important to her and to everybody in the gym at that moment. She took a deep breath to calm her nerves.

She didn't want to second-guess the Star City team, but she figured they would go to their best player—the tall outside hitter. Miki served the ball, this time well within bounds. A back row Star City player passed it to their setter.

Dina watched her body language. Out of the corner of her eye she saw Stephanie anticipate the set by going to the outside hitter. Dina almost took a step in that direction, but saw a subtle shift in the Star City setter's posture. Back set. She side stepped to her right. Bernadette was nowhere to be seen, so Dina would be flying solo.

Star City's opposite hitter soared into the air with her arm pulled back like a slingshot ready to pop. The tingles in Dina's stomach intensified as she leaped one-on-one against the strong Star City hitter. The ball rocketed toward Dina. She stretched her hands up and out as high and far as she could. The ball hit her right hand squarely and bounced back to the Star City side of the court. The libero dove for it. The ball hit the floor.

"We won," Stephanie screeched into her ear. She grabbed Dina in a hug and twirled her around.

The rest of their teammates joined the hug, and their momentum caused Dina and Stephanie to fall to the floor. Their teammates didn't seem to care and jumped on top.

After what seemed like twelve crushing hours, her teammates finally got off her. Dina sat on the floor, catching her breath.

Stephanie extended a hand. "C'mon, Stretch."

Dina grabbed the hand and leaped to her feet. "Thanks, boss." She let go and brushed off her spandex shorts.

"How does it feel to be getting a championship trophy today?" Stephanie grinned.

"Like we're the king of the mountain."

"King of the mountain," Stephanie said with a laugh. "I love it."

"Love what?" Miki fell in step as they approached the team bench.

Dina barely registered the conversation because she looked into the stands just in time to see Coach Blanchard from the West Lafayette Landsharks shaking hands with Christine. She watched as Christine's cheeks got redder and redder. Her heart swelled. It could mean only one thing. Christine was being asked to try out for the West Lafayette Landsharks next week, too.

Coach Blanchard stood up, shook hands with her parents, and then headed down the bleacher steps. Christine looked her way and shot her two thumbs up. Dina punched a fist in the air and laughed when Christine blew out a sigh of relief.

Dina sat back on the team bench and sighed. She'd thought her volleyball days had been over when she couldn't play in the games scheduled on Rosh Hashanah and Yom Kippur. If anything, missing those games made her appreciate the game even more. What she thought had been side outs against her had actually been side outs in her favor.

Epilogue

The *Fitness for Women*'s magazine reporter checked her digital recorder and pushed a lock of her graying dark brown hair behind an ear. She nodded for Dina to continue.

"Well," Dina said, "I think I really got hooked on volleyball when my family moved to Indiana. Here I was a twelve-year-old kid from Long Island, New York sent out to corn country. Thank goodness I made some friends really quickly at Earhart Middle School."

"And where are those friends now?"

"Now? Oh, Christine and I are still roommates."

"Christine Hannigan? Purdue's All-American libero?"

"Yeah, we were both seriously bummed when she didn't make the National team. She was this close." Dina held her thumb and index finger a half inch apart.

The reporter nodded. "She was one of the best liberos Purdue ever had. And you're an All-American yourself. One of the best middle blockers Purdue has ever seen, in my opinion."

"Oh, thanks." Dina felt herself blush. She squirmed on the locker room bench. She still wasn't used to all the attention that making the Olympic volleyball team brought her. She cleared her throat. "Christine will probably start student teaching in the fall."

"What grade?"

"Probably middle school. Social studies."

"Very cool. Will she coach, too?"

"She seriously wants to. She's so smart about the game."

The reporter smiled. "You were one of the most heavily recruited volleyball players out of high school your senior year. Why did you end up choosing Purdue?"

"Funny you should ask that. That first year I moved here,

Christine and I went to so many Purdue games that it made me fall in love with Purdue volleyball. The fans were so into it, and not only those crazy boilermaker students in the stands, but people from town, too. When Purdue took the court, the stands were always filled. And then I found out about the Big Ten Conference. Every year they sent a whole bunch of teams to the NCAA tournament. Funny thing is, my friend Brittany kept telling me you had to play for a California college if you wanted to play good volleyball, but I decided on Purdue. Brittany and I developed a serious rivalry over Purdue versus Stanford."

"Do you mean Brittany Nelson? Stanford's setter?"

"The one and the same."

"That must have been quite a middle school team you had back then." Dina could tell the reporter had just found a good angle for her story.

Dina nodded. "Back when I moved to Indiana, I remember thinking how great it would have been to play with Kristen Arthurs and Carrie Gurnell. Later on I learned about other Purdue superstars like Stephanie Lynch and Danita Merlau. It was quite a challenge following in their footsteps."

"What year did you move to Indiana?" The reporter made a notation on her note pad.

"Oh, uh, let's see. I was in seventh grade when we moved, so that would have been in the summer of 2009. Barack Obama's first year as president."

"Right." The reporter nodded. "That was the year Penn State barely beat Texas to take its third national title in a row, wasn't it?"

"Yeah, we were all at Christine's glued to the TV that December. Penn State went undefeated, 38-0, something like that. Nobody could touch them."

"Penn State has really made a name for itself," the reporter agreed. "So, let's talk about this summer's 2020 Olympics games. By all accounts, you'll be starting at middle blocker. Wait, how old are you again?"

"I'm twenty-two."

"That's right. You graduated from Purdue last spring." The reporter flipped back a few pages in her notepad. "You studied anthropology?"

Dina nodded. "I might get back to it someday, but for now my career is volleyball."

"So how did you get so good at the middle blocker position?"

Dina felt herself blush. "Well, somewhere along the way I learned how to read the setter's body language, so I knew where the set was going. And then I found I could jump pretty high to reach hits that other people couldn't."

"Being six foot four probably helps you with that."

"Yeah," Dina laughed, "but more importantly, way back in middle school, I learned how to deal with side outs that didn't go my way."

"Side outs?" The reporter clearly didn't understand.

Dina nodded. "Side outs that don't go your way are like when life throws you a challenge. You can't just fall apart, you have to deal with it. And, besides, the next side out will be in your favor."

"Very wise advice." The reporter scratched more notes on her pad.

She asked Dina a few more questions, but then one of the Olympic assistant coaches popped her head through the doorway.

"Dina?" Logan Tom said. "Sorry to interrupt, but we've got to get back on the bus."

"Okay, Coach. I'll be there in a sec."

Tom nodded and headed out of the locker room. The Olympic team had just finished playing an exhibition game against a group of college all-stars and had to get back on the road.

The reporter gestured toward the retreating coach. "I bet you've learned a few things from her, hmm?"

"Coach Tom? No kidding. She was my hero as a kid." Dina stood up. "She still is."

The reporter stood up as well. She put out her hand. "Dina, I hope most of the side outs in your life go your way."

"Thanks. You, too." Dina shook hands with the reporter, picked up her volleyball bag, and headed toward the bus that was taking them to another U.S. city for another pre-Olympic exhibition game.

ABOUT THE AUTHOR

Barbara L. Clanton is a native New Yorker who left those "New York minutes" for the slower-paced palm-tree-filled life in Orlando, Florida. While still in school she played any sport she could find: softball, volleyball, basketball, and field hockey. During high school, she could even be found in the upstairs gym playing team handball with her friends. She played softball at Princeton and was the captain her senior year. She currently teaches mathematics at a college preparatory school in the Orlando area and has coached both softball and basketball in both New York and Florida. She still plays softball, but has picked up a new hobby! "Dr. Barb" plays bass guitar in a pop-rock band called The Flounders. Her writing credits so far include four young adult novels from Regal Crest Enterprises, LLC. *Out of Left Field: Marlee's Story*, *Art for Art's Sake: Meredith's Story*, *Quite an Undertaking: Devon's Story*, and *Tools of Ignorance: Lisa's Story*. *Bases Loaded* is her other Title IX novel from Dragonfeather Books. Visit her website at www.BLClanton.com.